Jimmy's face was radiant as he stood onstage in the Christmas play, and said, "Do you see the star?"

A surge of love overwhelmed Evan. He hadn't thought he had that much love left in him after he'd lost his wife and son. But his heart told him there was room for Jimmy.

Evan made his way to where he had seen Chloe sitting. Jimmy ran from the stage straight to her. She knelt, giving him a huge hug. Getting closer, he could hear her praising his performance. "You were the very best one!"

He bounced on his sneakers. "Really?"

"Really!" She hugged him again. "The very, very, very best."

Jimmy hugged her back hard before finally letting go.

"You haven't told me what you want for Christmas yet, big guy."

"A family."

She leaned her head against his. "Me, too."

Evan was struck by their words. The star on the stage twinkled, beaconing its message of hope. And he wondered if he dared believe.

Books by Bonnie K. Winn

Love Inspired

*A Family All Her Own
*Family Ties
*Promise of Grace
*Protected Hearts
*Child of Mine
*To Love Again
*Lone Star Blessings
*Return to Rosewood
*Jingle Bell Blessings

*Rosewood, Texas

BONNIE K. WINN

is a hopeless romantic who has written incessantly since the third grade. So it seems only natural that she turned to romance writing. A seasoned author of historical and contemporary romance, Bonnie has won numerous awards for her bestselling books. *Affaire de Coeur* chose her as one of the Top Ten Romance Writers in America.

Bonnie loves writing contemporary romance because she can set her stories in the modern cities close to her heart and explore the endlessly fascinating strengths of today's women.

Living in the foothills of the Rockies gives her plenty of inspiration and a touch of whimsy, as well. She shares her life with her husband, son and a spunky Norwich terrier who lends his characteristics to many pets in her stories. Bonnie's keeping mum about anyone else's characteristics she may have borrowed.

Jingle Bell Blessings
Bonnie K. Winn

Steeple
Hill®

Published by Steeple Hill Books™

STEEPLE HILL BOOKS

Steeple
Hill®

Recycling programs
for this product may
not exist in your area.

ISBN-13: 978-0-373-81517-3

JINGLE BELL BLESSINGS

Copyright © 2010 by Bonnie K. Winn

www.SteepleHill.com

Printed in U.S.A.

Behold, children are a gift of the Lord.
—*Psalms* 127:3

For our beautiful Liberty Winn
Born April 18, 2010

Chapter One

Chloe Reed gripped little Jimmy's hand as much to stop her own shaking as to reassure him. Everything was on the line. The boy's future, her own. Swallowing, she tentatively raised the brass knocker on the massive front door.

Silence.

She bent down to encourage Jimmy, and whispered, "It'll be okay, I promise."

The door whipped open suddenly and she nearly teetered. Unnerved, she looked up, way up, to meet a dark pair of unpleased eyes. Set in a rugged face with a determined chin, his eyes swept over her in uncompromising dismissal.

Awkwardly, Chloe straightened up, expecting to meet him face-to-face, but he was tall, unusually tall. "Um...hello."

"Yes?"

"I'm here to see Evan Mitchell."

"You're looking at him."

"Oh." She'd held a wild hope that she'd knocked on the wrong door. Despite her boss's warnings, she had wanted to believe that Evan Mitchell would be approachable, reasonable. "I'm Chloe Reed." Wishing she could shield the little boy, she squeezed his hand again. "And this is Jimmy Mitchell."

Eyebrows as dark as the man's thick hair swooped downward. "What are you doing here?"

Wanting to protect the seven-year-old, Chloe beseeched the man with a pleading glance.

Relenting, Evan opened the door wider. "Come in."

She and Jimmy both stared as they walked into the circular, two-story-high entry hall, their steps echoing on the marble floor of the impressive house.

Evan hadn't expected his late cousin's son to appear on his doorstop, but he didn't want to hurt the boy. Raising his voice, he called for the housekeeper. "Thelma! Can you come out here?"

Wiping her hands on a cheery gingham apron, a pert woman in her sixties dashed into the hall. "What is it? I'm in the middle of pie making and..." Her voice trailed off when she saw Chloe and the boy, her face easing into a smile. "Who do we have here?"

"Spencer's boy," Evan replied briefly.

Thelma's eyes widened, then warmed in understanding as she spoke to Jimmy. "Do you like apple pie?"

Uncertain in his new surroundings, Jimmy looked at her warily, taking a step backward, leaning against Chloe.

Thelma walked toward him, extending her hand. "I've got lemon meringue, pumpkin, cherry and banana cream, too. I sure could use a taster."

Jimmy looked up at Chloe, who nodded. Accepting Thelma's hand, the pair disappeared in the direction of the kitchen.

Evan wished he could whisk the woman away as easily, but he knew that wasn't going to happen. Instead he gestured toward the parlor, observing the swing of her long, wavy, caramel-colored hair as she walked. Once in the room, she turned, her large green eyes questioning.

"Have a seat."

As she did, he wondered what his late cousin's attorney was up to now. Sending a pretty woman was novel, even for Holden Wainwright.

"Miss…?"

"Reed," she supplied nervously. "Chloe. Call me Chloe, please. I work for Holden Wainwright. I'm his…that is, I'm the estate representative for Jimmy's parents."

He'd guessed as much. "What are you doing here?"

"Mr. Wainwright wants what's best for Jimmy. Your cousin and his wife didn't have any immediate family who could take care of him. And Mr.

Wainwright himself is an old bachelor—he doesn't have a clue about raising a young boy. That leaves you."

"Wainwright knows how I feel about that."

Her face filled with distress, darkening her already unusual eyes, pulling down the edges of her full lips. "He does?"

"Oh, come now, Miss Reed—"

"Chloe," she corrected, staring at him in shock.

"Miss Reed, we aren't going to get to know each other well enough to worry about first names. I told Wainwright I wasn't going to change my mind. And I'm not." The thought of growing close to another child... The pain nearly choked off his breath. And his voice was gruffer than usual because of it. "You've come on a fool's errand. I can't say whether you're Wainwright's pawn or a schemer yourself. Doesn't matter. You can sort that out with Wainwright when you're back in Milwaukee."

Chloe found her voice. "It's taken us forever to get out here. The flight from Milwaukee to San Antonio took two plane changes. Then driving way out here to Rosewood...and you expect us to just turn around and head back?" Some of her distress had vanished, leaving fire in its place. "And I'm supposed to tell Jimmy what? That the only relative he has on this continent doesn't even want to get to know him?"

Evan watched as the quivering in her neck spread to the hollow at the base of her throat.

She stood abruptly, pressing her hands together. "How do you live with yourself?"

Bleakly. "We aren't in the time of Dickens, Miss Reed. There are no workhouses, no orphanages. Spencer left the boy a trust fund that'll guarantee his future."

"The *boy's* name is Jimmy. And all the money in the world can't replace his parents." She gestured toward the rest of the comfortable room. "Since your father is alive and living here, you obviously can't understand that kind of trauma."

Evan's throat was so tight it was a wonder any oxygen could pass into his lungs. *Trauma.* A trendy term, like *closure.* As though such a thing existed. The hole in his heart would never heal, certainly never close. Not since he'd lost Robin and Sean. He crossed the room so he could look out the tall, wide window. A rental car was parked in the circular drive. So that much was true. "And what do you know about trauma, Miss Reed?"

"Enough," she replied evenly.

Turning his back to the faceted panes of glass, he watched the sunshine illuminate Chloe's face. Wainwright was playing hardball. Sending a woman Evan couldn't ignore. At least that's what the old horse trader thought. "I doubt that. What are you, twenty-four, twenty-five?"

"Actually, I'm twenty-seven. But—"

He held up one hand. "No need to get in a one-upmanship contest. Not even the most tragic tale's going to change my mind, Miss Reed. I'm surprised you didn't learn more about the situation before you agreed to bring Jimmy here. I haven't seen Spencer since we were teenagers. Hardly a close relationship that would warrant any reason to appoint me the boy's guardian."

"Jimmy," she emphasized. "And to repeat myself, Jimmy doesn't have anyone else." Chloe took a breath. "He's alone. You're his parents' choice as guardian. Have you no compassion?"

Evan met the woman's unrelenting stare. His compassion had drowned along with Robin and Sean. But he didn't feel the need to spill those details to a stranger. The deaths of his wife and son were sacred, not to be bandied about for this woman's benefit.

Chloe stood as well, crossing the room, planting her petite frame in front of his. "I'm not suggesting it's an easy obligation. But surely you can see the sense in having Jimmy stay for a while, to see if the arrangement will work." She steepled her fingers together, the criss-cross pressure making them whiten. "The estate will pay for my services during the transition."

His humorless chuckle was bitingly sarcastic. "Two for the price of one? Am I supposed to believe that's a good deal?"

Thunder clashed across her face and for a moment it looked as though she was about to launch a tirade.

Instead, she tugged at the jacket of her prim, navy blue suit, then tightened her hands further. "I don't believe you should be thinking of Jimmy in terms of a deal. But if that's the only emotional barometer you possess, then I'll tell you that it is a first-rate deal. Jimmy's kind, unspoiled, loving. And he's just had both of his parents blown to smithereens in a factory explosion."

Not stopping to let him speak, she held up her hands, ticking off her points. "One grandfather's dead. One grandmother is in a nursing home with Alzheimer's. His other set of grandparents are on a dig in Egypt and suggested we put him in a boarding school.

"You knew Spencer. Do you think he'd want his son to have the same kind of lonely life he did? Crying himself to sleep because the other boys went home to their families for holidays and he stayed behind, hurt and alone? Spencer told Mr. Wainwright that his only good memories of growing up were here, in Rosewood, with you and your family. Don't you think his son deserves to be happy?"

Evan's gaze narrowed, his suspicions growing as he studied her. "Sounds like you're pretty chummy with Wainwright."

"I'm in his employ. You should know that Mr. Wainwright was more than Spencer's attorney. He and Spencer's father were best friends. After Spencer's father died a few years ago, Mr. Wainwright did his best to step into a father's role, to give Spencer *some* semblance of a parent."

Evan still didn't know what she had to gain by talking him into a guardianship, but it wasn't going to happen. "Then perhaps he ought to step into the grandparent role now."

She quieted for a moment, then her ocean-green eyes held a clashing combination of sadness and ferocity. "Mr. Wainwright's health is not…" Chloe took another breath. "He's had heart problems—three surgeries so far. He doesn't think it would be fair to Jimmy to take him in and then…" Clearing her throat, she met his gaze. "And regardless of his health, Mr. Wainwright doesn't know anything about little boys. He's never had children of his own. However, he does know that Jimmy needs more than an ailing elderly acquaintance or a soulless boarding school to be happy."

Evan knew the amount of love little boys needed. He didn't want or need a reminder. Five-year-old Sean had filled his heart and life. The emptiness was a piercing, never-ending reminder. Looking away from Chloe, he saw the shadows on the front lawn lengthening. Chloe could hardly drive to San Antonio in the fast-approaching darkness. And Rosewood's only bed-and-breakfast was full because of the approaching holidays.

Holidays. Little boys and holidays. The combination used to fill him with joy. Now the dread was inescapable. Still, he couldn't, in good conscience, turn Spencer's boy and this woman out in the night. "Dinner should be ready in about an hour. Thelma will show you to a guest room."

Chloe's delicate features brightened.

"Just for the night," Evan cautioned. "I haven't changed my mind and I'm not going to." Wainwright could send a dozen beautiful women and it wouldn't matter. His ability to love a child had died with his son. And there was no resurrecting it.

Chloe found herself tiptoeing as she wandered past the entry hall. After Evan Mitchell's rather abrupt dismissal, she wasn't quite sure what to do with herself. He had mentioned dinner and staying the night. Should she bring in their suitcases? No, she told herself. Plunking them on the floor of the immaculate entry or parlor seemed like a terrible idea, especially since hers was a Salvation Army classic. And she wasn't sure where the back entrance was.

Jimmy hadn't emerged since the kind-looking woman had led him away. The scent of sweet fruit and browning pie crust melded with savory vegetables and something else. Beef? Maybe it was stew.

Chloe's stomach growled. "Just like one of Pavlov's dogs," she muttered to herself. She could read a highway sign announcing the next Dairy Queen and suddenly be swamped with a craving for ice cream.

"Chloe?" Jimmy questioned, his voice floating out from deeper in the house. Even from the distance, she could hear the anxiety coating his words.

"We're in the kitchen," Thelma added in a louder voice. "Down the hall to the left. Just pass through the dining room."

Chloe followed her directions, pushing open a swinging door at the end of a long passageway. For a moment she thought she'd stumbled into the kitchen of the Keebler elves. Bright bursts of color caught her attention, pulling her gaze to the limestone counters, the cozy eating nook, the massive stove.

Several pies cooled on the wood sideboard in front of the slightly opened window. Despite the charm of the room, Chloe wanted only to see Jimmy, to make sure he was all right.

She placed an arm over his shoulders. "How we doing, big guy?"

He scooted close to her without replying.

And Chloe wished she could make everything better for him.

"That young man is a super worker," Thelma told her, winking at Jimmy. "Helped me roll out the pie dough."

Chloe squeezed his shoulder. "That's great, Jimmy! I've never been able to make a decent pie crust."

"Cold water's the secret," Thelma continued as though they were old acquaintances. "Ice cold.

Otherwise the shortening melts down, makes it tough and the crust falls apart."

"I'll try to remember that." She bent down, closer to Jimmy. "You getting hungry?"

"I'm afraid I've given him quite a few samples of the pie fillings," Thelma confessed. "I knew something was off with the banana cream. So we had to taste that one at least three or four times."

"It was good," Jimmy finally offered.

"It smells delicious," Chloe agreed with a smile for the older woman. "Do you always make this many pies at a time?"

"We have a bake sale every year to raise money for the Angel Tree." She paused, then quieted her voice. "It's for the holidays, you know."

Chloe guessed the fund was to buy toys for children who wouldn't get them otherwise. And she appreciated Thelma's discretion around Jimmy. He'd had more than his share of untimely discoveries.

"Since Evan didn't introduce us, I'm Thelma, the housekeeper. My husband, Ned, is the…well… he's pretty much the everything-else man. Keeps up the gardens, the cars, whatever needs fixing."

"I'm Chloe Reed. I work for Holden Wainwright."

Thelma started to reach out her hand, then realized it was covered in flour. "Pleased to meet you. And I've thoroughly enjoyed meeting Jimmy. Ned's eaten so many of my pies over the years, he automatically says they taste good no matter what I put in them. The Mitchell men don't like their pies too sweet and Jimmy here helped me balance out the lemon meringue."

Jimmy wasn't distracted, though. His expression was pensive, anxious, worried. And Chloe felt sure he must be exhausted. As kind as Thelma seemed, she was another stranger.

"Would you mind if we walk around the grounds?" Chloe queried.

"Fresh air might do you both good." Thelma dusted the flour from her hands, then wiped them on her apron. "Back door's right over here. You'll find doors in most every room on this level—French doors open out from the front room. And upstairs, there's even a door that leads out and down the staircase from the bedrooms. There's three sets of stairs in the house." She pointed to the one in the kitchen. "We call this one the back stairs. Used to be just for the servants. As for all the doors, I guess a few hundred years ago people felt they might need to get away in a hurry." She chuckled. "There I go, running off at the mouth. Takes a little while to get the feel of the place, but then it seems right homey."

"I'm sure it is," Chloe agreed, edging toward the door.

Thelma smiled. "There's a nice swing out back. Actually two. One on the porch, another under the oak tree. Can't miss either."

"Thank you." Chloe still gripped Jimmy's hand

as they stepped outside. The air was clean, tinged with the faint aroma of burning leaves. She guessed that out in the country people didn't have to worry so much about air pollution.

"Let's find the one under the tree," Chloe suggested. As Thelma had said, it was easy to see the glider swing. It sat beneath a tall oak tree that had already lost many of its leaves. Jimmy clung to her hand as she guided him to the cozy-looking spot.

Once seated, Chloe gently urged the glider into motion. "We can rest before dinner if you'd like to."

"Then what?"

Immediately, she wondered if the child had guessed or overheard Evan's intentions. "Then we'll be all stuffed and we'll get a good night's sleep."

"Here?"

"Sure, big guy. That's where we are."

Shoulders hunched, Jimmy's head dropped forward, his shiny hair nearly obscuring still-childish features. "I like sleeping in my own room."

A room he would never again occupy. The house was being sold, along with the majority of its contents. Only photos and sentimental items were being boxed up for storage. All of Jimmy's life, all of his memories. The thought dried her throat, stung her eyes. But Jimmy didn't need sympathy. He needed someone strong to lean on. If that wasn't going to be Evan Mitchell, that left only her. Despite being solely responsible for her mother's care, Chloe couldn't abandon this boy. Even if it meant taking on a forceful, obstinate man like Evan Mitchell.

Dinner was more formal and somber than Chloe expected. Thelma served them in the dining room, then retreated to the kitchen to eat dinner with her husband. And Evan Mitchell wasn't a very entertaining host. He sat at the head of the table, while she and Jimmy faced each other across the long, banquet-sized table.

Thelma had served them each generous helpings of stew, along with freshly baked biscuits.

"Thelma's oven must stay busy," Chloe ventured. "She was making pies and now these biscuits."

"Umm," Evan replied so sparsely, he might not have even spoken.

Chloe smiled encouragingly at Jimmy, then tried again. "I understood that your father lived here with you."

"It's the family home. We share it."

"Isn't he joining us?"

Evan looked annoyed by her questions. "He's hunting quail with friends out near the Markham ranch. They make a day and night of it."

Chloe dipped her spoon into the savory stew. "This is delicious. Don't you think so, Jimmy?"

He scrunched his narrow shoulders together, the sweep of his dark hair hiding his eyes. "Guess so."

Trying to lighten the glum atmosphere, Chloe took some butter for her biscuit. "Have Thelma and her husband been with you long?"

"Curious, aren't you?" Evan replied. Then he glanced over at Jimmy. "They've been here as long as I can remember."

"Came with the house?" she questioned, hoping to infuse some cheer into the conversation.

Evan looked at her as though she'd suggested swallowing a bucket of mud.

"Just kidding, of course," she tried to remedy. "I haven't had any experience with household employees."

"They're not just employees," he replied sharply. "They're family."

Chastened, Chloe stirred her spoon aimlessly. "Of course." If not for Jimmy, she would have fervently wished for a hole to appear in the floor so she could vanish.

Silence reigned, interrupted only by the scrape of spoons against the bowls. The clinking of china when a coffee cup was returned to its saucer. The last time Chloe had felt this uncomfortable at a dinner table, she'd been twelve years old and painfully aware of the boy sitting across from her. He was fourteen and she had a terrible crush on him. In turn, he considered her a complete nuisance. Seemed she hadn't progressed much from then.

Thelma eventually cleared their dishes and then

brought in dessert plates. "Lemon meringue," she announced. "Had some good help making this one. Wasn't hard to decide which one to keep for dessert."

Jimmy glanced at the housekeeper, a furtive, slightly pleased look.

Thelma winked back at him.

Chloe wished the width of the table weren't so broad. She would have liked to squeeze his hand in encouragement. Instead, she smiled at him. Lifting her gaze she caught Evan studying them.

He didn't blink. The woman didn't act like a mere estate representative. Which made him that much more distrustful. Evidently, she stood to profit if she convinced him to accept the guardianship. Wainwright had the funds.

And the old guy had always held a soft spot for Spencer. After the explosion in their newly refurbished factory, Spencer's wishes had been presented. And Wainwright had pled his case as though Spencer were a son rather than the son of a friend.

Committed to placing Jimmy in the Mitchell home, Wainwright may have offered Chloe quite a sum to succeed. Why else would the woman have traveled across the country with no guarantee of how she would be received?

* * *

Thelma rustled around the large bedroom as Chloe stared first at the tall ceilings, then the intricate moldings and charming bay window. She gently touched the delicate lace curtains as she admired the four-poster bed and marble-topped dresser. "The room's lovely," she murmured. "It's really a guest room?"

"Evan's mother decorated every room on this floor. The men didn't want her changing the rustic stuff in the den and the parlor's stayed pretty much the same for generations."

"She's passed away, hasn't she? Evan's mother?"

Thelma stopped plumping the pillow she held. "Adele died... several years ago, now. And..." She stopped abruptly.

Chloe knew that Evan was single. Mr. Wainwright had given her a brief sketch about him. Evan ran the family business, in fact, devoted all of his time to it. Could that be why he was so insistent about not taking on Jimmy?

Thelma laid the pillow at the head of the bed, then checked the growing flames in the fireplace. "Gets chilly this time of year. Family had central heat installed back when Mr. Gordon, Evan's father, was a boy. But when the wind's howling, it's awful nice to have a fire."

Standing next to a wide chaise that was angled by the fireplace, Chloe agreed. "I love a good fire and I haven't had a fireplace of my own in… well, a long time." *Not since the family home had to be sold.*

Thelma crossed the room to an archway containing a door. "This opens into Jimmy's room. It used to be the nursery."

Chloe peeked inside, seeing that he was still fascinated by the interesting little room with its slanted ceiling, nooks, arches and cushioned window seat that overlooked the widow's walk surrounding the upper story. "He may have trouble sleeping tonight. He's had a lot of… changes."

"Mr. Gordon told me all about Jimmy when the lawyer wrote. Poor little tyke. We all hoped Evan…" Thelma sighed. "Mr. Gordon's too old to take on raising the boy himself. Wouldn't be right for Jimmy if…well, if Mr. Gordon couldn't see him all the way through 'til he's old enough to be on his own."

Chloe thought she heard a thread of worry in the woman's voice. "Is Mr. Mitchell ill?"

Thelma shook her head. "He wouldn't retire until a few years ago. Worked hard all his life. Too hard. A boy needs parents who can keep up with him."

"That's how Mr. Wainwright feels, too. When I'm taking care of Jimmy, I have to stay on top speed myself."

A knowing smile lit Thelma's eyes. "I'm guessing you don't mind that too much."

"He's a wonderful little boy." So much so that Chloe knew she would have to rein in her feelings. A huge part of her wished she could just take him back to Milwaukee, raise him as her own. And that was impossible. "Thelma, would it be too much trouble to make some hot cocoa?"

"Course not. I'll bring it up directly."

She didn't want to cause the woman more work. "I'm happy to come and get it."

Waving her hands in dismissal, Thelma tsked. "Don't want to hear another word about it. You just get the little one settled."

Chloe exhaled in relief. Thelma was proving to be an ally. "Thanks." As Thelma left, Chloe knocked lightly on the connecting door frame to Jimmy's room. "Mind if I come in?"

"Uh-uh." Jimmy sat on the edge of the bed, staring out the large window. Still dressed in his best clothes, as though waiting for something that would never happen, he looked completely, inescapably alone.

"Know what I was thinking?" she asked in an encouraging voice.

He shook his head.

"We could get in our jammies, scrunch up on this amazing chair in front of the fireplace in my room and tell stories." Chloe wriggled her eyebrows. "Might even be some hot cocoa in the deal."

"My dad used to read me a story every night and Mommy would sing."

Chloe sat down beside him, putting her arm around

his shoulders. "You know, I seem to remember packing a few of your favorite books."

Leaving him to change into his pajamas, Chloe did the same. By the time she'd tied the sash on her thick, fluffy robe, she heard a light knock on the door. Expecting Thelma, she whipped open the door with a smile.

Evan Mitchell's muscular frame filled the doorway and his forbidding expression sent her smile plummeting.

"If you need anything," he began uncomfortably. "Just ask Thelma."

Chloe clutched her pink robe, excruciatingly aware of the matching bunny slippers on her feet. Trying to tuck them backward just pulled his attention toward the embarrassing footwear.

Straightening her shoulders, she tried to look as businesslike as possible. "We're fine, thank you."

He didn't reply.

Unnerved, she tried to think of something else to say, to distract him, to remove his all-too-male presence. "Thelma's making us some hot cocoa."

"Right." He glanced down the empty corridor.

Chloe fervently wished Thelma would make an appearance.

But the hall remained empty.

"I'll say good night then," Evan finished.

"Good night." Rattled, Chloe shut the door and retreated to the burgundy velvet chaise. Not that she needed the heat from the fire. Touching her cheeks, she confirmed they were warm and no doubt bright red. Oh, yes. Evan Mitchell had seen past her professional facade. All the way to her pink bunny slippers.

Chapter Two

The fire was dying down and their cups of cocoa were empty. Chloe had read three of Jimmy's books, told him several of her favorite stories and he was finally nodding off. It had been an eternally long day for her. She could only imagine how it had tired him. But the little guy didn't complain. Instead, he had cuddled close on the chaise, listening to the stories, and trying to stay awake.

Certain that he was ready for bed, she scooped him up from the lounger.

"I'm not sleepy," he mumbled, his head falling on her shoulder.

"I know, big guy. We'll just rest for a while." Chloe carried him through the adjoining door into the nursery. Thelma had made up both the child's bed and the single bed nearby. Chloe gently deposited him on the smaller bed. Then she grabbed his stuffed dog, Elbert, and laid it close. Pulling the sheet and handmade quilt up to his chin, she kept her voice low. "Snug as a bug in a rug."

Jimmy's eyelids were drifting closed, but he struggled to keep them open. "Don't go."

"Okay." She sat on the edge of his bed, softly singing one of the Irish lullabies her mother had sung to her when she was little.

Chloe hummed the chorus again, watching until finally the gentle rise and fall of his chest told her that Jimmy had nodded off. Quietly she returned to her room, leaving the door to the nursery open. Warmed by the dwindling fire, she crossed over to the bay window. Old-fashioned streetlights—that she guessed had been converted from oil—softly illuminated the brick-paved street below. She hadn't imagined such quaint places still existed. As she studied the engaging landscape, she spotted a lone figure walking up the lane. When the man reached the Mitchell home he turned and headed to the tall oak on the knolled rise of the lawn.

Unable to take her eyes from the man, she glimpsed his face when he stepped beside the gas light in the yard. Evan Mitchell. She shouldn't be surprised. After all, it was his home. Continuing to watch, she saw him sit on a stone bench that curved around the tree. Evan just didn't seem like the sort of man to take solitary nighttime walks. Fleetingly she wondered if he was cold.

Not that it should matter to her. His behavior had

been utterly frigid. Still, she wondered why he sat alone, what drove him out in the chilly night. Wisps of clouds drifted, allowing some moonlight to filter downward. Evan looked up in the direction of the light. His expression was so bleak, Chloe's hand flew to her mouth to stop an automatic cry of distress. What was troubling him so deeply?

Not that he would confide in her. Nor should she want him to. Evan was the enemy, the man who decided Jimmy's fate. But the part of her that always reached out to others refused to stay quiet. Was it possible that Evan had issues that she needed to learn? Issues he had to resolve before accepting a child in his life?

The questions stilled. Because Evan Mitchell dropped his head in his hands. And Chloe couldn't intrude on his private moment any longer.

Even though the soft feather bed was incredibly comfortable, Chloe couldn't sleep. Literally tossing and shifting in the bed, she'd twisted the sheets and lace crocheted coverlet into a tangled mess. But sleep was impossible with the mass of conflicting thoughts racing through her mind. Hearing a sudden cry, she bolted upright. Remembering the small set of wooden stairs beside the mattress for climbing in and out of the tall bed, she clicked on her lamp so she could find them. Untangling herself from the covers, she grabbed her robe and raced into the adjoining room.

Jimmy was sitting up in the bed, looking terrified.

Immediately, Chloe reached out to pull him into her arms. Rocking him back and forth, she imparted all the comfort she possessed. "It's okay," she murmured. "You're safe. I'm right here." He shook with a convulsed sob and Chloe's eyes filled. If only she could take his pain for him. Rubbing his back, she held him until he was finally still. Pulling back slightly, she smoothed the dark hair from his forehead. "Was it a dream?"

He nodded, a jerky motion. "And when I woke up I didn't know where I was."

"I wasn't having much luck sleeping either. I'd probably go to sleep faster if I wasn't alone." She rubbed her chin as though in deep concentration. "Do you suppose I could sleep on the extra bed in here? It would really help me out."

This time when he nodded, he looked up at her with relief in his big brown eyes.

She eased the tears from his cheeks with her fingers. "I know I'll feel safe in here with you."

He sniffled.

"Okay, better get that bug snug again." He dutifully laid back down and she tucked him in. "If it wouldn't keep you awake, I'd kind of like to keep the little light on."

"It's okay," he agreed gratefully.

She smoothed his hair once more. "Thanks."

Climbing into the bed she guessed once belonged to a nanny, Chloe actually did feel better. She had been worried about Jimmy being alone, frightened in the strange house. She smoothed the blanket in place, leaving her arms out. Now, if she could just get Evan Mitchell out of her thoughts. Sighing, she realized that wouldn't be nearly as easy.

Early morning sunlight invaded Chloe's face. Scrunching her eyes, she reached for the sheet to cover them. Awareness hit at the same instant. Immediately, she looked at Jimmy's bed. It was empty. Fear filled her chest. Surely he hadn't run away. He didn't know anyone in Rosewood.

Blinking, she focused again and saw his pajamas thrown across the bed. Next to them was his stuffed dog, Elbert. Jimmy wouldn't have left his treasured friend behind.

Although reassured, she dressed quickly so she could look for him. Evan Mitchell wouldn't welcome a curious, roaming child in his house.

Once downstairs, she headed toward the kitchen, but paused when she heard voices in the dining room. Walking slowly, she approached the group.

"You must be Chloe," a gray-haired man boomed in a deep voice. He stood up, keeping Jimmy close to his side. "I'm Gordon Mitchell, Evan's father. Sure pleased to have you here."

Surreptitiously glancing around, she didn't see Evan, and relaxed. "Thank you."

Thelma poured another mug of coffee and handed it to Chloe. "Morning. How'd you sleep?"

"Very well, thanks. It's a beautiful room." She glanced at Gordon. "A beautiful house."

"Too empty, though." He patted Jimmy's shoulder. "Need some young energy to fill it up again."

Unwilling to discuss Evan's refusal in front of Jimmy, Chloe sipped the bracing brew.

Jimmy knelt down. "Did you see the dog, Chloe?"

A calm golden retriever seemed delighted by Jimmy's attention, waving a beautifully plumed tail and pushing his muzzle into Jimmy's hand.

"I don't remember seeing him yesterday," she mused.

"Bailey was with me," Gordon explained. "Hunting. But he pined for Evan the whole time."

"He's Evan's dog?" Chloe asked in surprise.

"Bailey's usually camped out by Evan's side, clinging like thistle. Jimmy's pretty special to have tempted him away."

"French toast this morning." Thelma winked at Jimmy. "Thought I might find somebody who'd like it."

"Sounds great." Chloe slipped into a chair. "How did your hunting trip go, Mr. Mitchell?"

"Best part of it is the guys. We tell the same stories we've told each other for the last fifty years, and now that we're getting on, some of 'em even sound new again." His dark eyes crinkled with kindness.

Although she could see the resemblance between the two generations of men, Gordon exuded warmth, friendliness. Chloe wanted to relax, but she was still facing a major confrontation.

The thought apparently conjured up the man in question. Evan stalked into the room, crossing over to the sideboard to pour a mug of coffee. Bailey jumped up and ran to his side. Evan rubbed the dog's head. As he did, Evan turned, his gaze narrowing first on Chloe, then Jimmy and finally his father.

Thelma pushed open the door from the kitchen, holding a large platter. She placed the French toast in the middle of the table. "Eat it while it's hot."

Chloe turned to Jimmy. "Looks good, doesn't it?" Hoping Evan wouldn't open with an argument, she speared one piece.

Gordon passed the pitcher of warm syrup. "Thelma dusts the toast in powdered sugar, but I still like my maple syrup. How 'bout you, Jimmy?"

"I like syrup," he replied in a tiny voice.

Knowing Jimmy was nervous, she patted his leg. "Me, too."

Evan continued to stare at his father.

Gordon met his son's gaze, his voice deceptively casual. "I was just about to invite Chloe and Jimmy to stay for a while. Won't be long 'til Thanksgiving. Holidays are always better with children, more family."

A vein in Evan's muscular neck bulged, while his lips thinned into an angry line. He pushed back his chair, scraping it loudly over the wide planked floor as he rose. "I have to get to work."

His boots rang loudly as he left, and the sound of the door slamming echoed through the house. Bailey whined, then laid down next to the front door, apparently waiting for his master.

"Did I make him mad?" Jimmy asked in an even smaller voice.

"Of course not!" Chloe rushed to reassure him. "He probably has problems at work that are on his mind, that's all." She glanced at Gordon. "It's a family business, isn't it?"

Gordon nodded. "Mitchell Stone. My great-grandfather started the quarry with not much more than a land claim and a box of dynamite. A few men agreed to work with him in exchange for shares in the company. A lot of their descendants are fourth-generation employees now."

Chloe glanced upward at the elegant chandelier, just one of the impressive fixtures in the obviously expensive home. "So your family built all this up themselves?"

He chuckled softly. "First house wasn't much more than a tar shack. The way I heard it, my great-grandmother threatened to dig enough stone out of the quarry herself to build a decent house. But in time, they built a small wood cottage—it's the carriage house we use for a garage now."

"I think Thelma mentioned that you're retired?"

"Yep. Evan's in charge now."

Chloe swallowed, hating to pry, but needing to know as much as possible about Evan. "Is that a good thing?"

"He lives and breathes work. Since the recession, Evan's done everything he can to keep the place together so no one loses their jobs. It's a Mitchell trait, I suppose." Gordon absently tapped his fingers against the tabletop. "Feeling responsible. Can't let go when…"

Chloe waited quietly.

But Gordon glanced up, reined in his memories and lifted a mug of coffee. "So, it's settled. You and Jimmy will stay here. I'd like to show you around town. See the school, the church. People are friendly in Rosewood. Not much like a big city."

"Milwaukee's not small, but it is down to earth," Chloe replied. "Kind of the best between a small town and a big city."

"You have family there?"

Chloe nodded, thinking of her mother, worrying

about her. "My father passed away when I was in junior high school. My younger brother, Chip, is in the army—he and his family are stationed in Germany. And my mother lives in an extended care facility. She has COPD—it's a chronic pulmonary condition. Because of it, she can't live on her own. If she had a bad episode and no one was around, it could be..." she glanced down at Jimmy, then up to meet the understanding in Gordon's eyes. "Since I work full-time, it's safest where she is."

"Much extended family?"

"They all live pretty far away in the rural part of the state. But Milwaukee still clings to its ethnic roots. We have areas that are primarily German, Romanian, Hungarian. Makes neighborhoods friendly."

"Sounds familiar."

"Rosewood has neighborhoods like that?"

He smiled. "Pretty much the whole town. We're a dying breed, but we don't cotton to superstores, tourist traps. So far, we've been able to keep them out. The news always says mom-and-pop businesses can't survive, but they do here." Gordon chuckled. "Sounds like I'm about a century old with my reminiscing."

Chloe was liking him more and more. "I noticed the town was pretty when we were driving through." She lowered her lashes, trying to hide some of her anxiety from Jimmy. "But I was too nervous...driving in an unfamiliar rental car to pay very much attention."

"Then we need to take care of that." He turned to Jimmy, who was adding even more syrup to his plate. "What do you say? After breakfast, we check things out?"

Jimmy appeared shy but pleased.

While she was looking forward to their tour, Chloe didn't know how it was going to help matters. The look in Evan's eyes that morning had said it all. He wasn't about to change his mind.

Evan studied the latest financial report. Mitchell Stone was sinking as though pummeled by its own boulders.

Perry Perkin, their chief financial officer, shoved both hands in his pockets. "Numbers won't get any better by staring at them."

"Yeah." But he had to turn around the profits. The employees depended on him, most were like family. "Construction business is picking up. Got two new orders this week."

"Small ones. Evan, you know they aren't going to carry the payroll."

"Recession hit everyone, Perry. It'll take time for bigger deals to roll in." Mitchell Stone had operations all over the hill country and in other parts of the state. Even though most of Texas hadn't been hit as hard by the recession as the rest of the country, new construction was still down. And many of their orders had been national as well as international, customers that still remained on shaky ground. "We'll make the payroll."

"If you keep putting your personal money in the business, you'll tank when it does."

"*If,* not when." Evan plowed his fingers through his hair, then looked out the window at Main Street. "You know we've had our offices in this building more than a century. My great-grandfather didn't want to confine himself to one quarry, so he insisted on having an office right in the middle of town. That's why he kept looking for more sources, staking more claims all his life. Then my grandfather and my father. And there was a little thing called the Great Depression that happened along the way. But Mitchell Stone never closed its doors. I don't intend to let it happen on my watch."

Perry was empathetic but realistic. "You know as well as I do, that the first decade of this millennium wasn't hit by just a recession. It was a depression."

"Plattville is accepting bids next month on their new courthouse. If we can get a lock on who wins the job…" Speculating, Evan knew Mitchell Stone would be one of dozens interested in supplying the limestone.

Perry sighed. "Look, I've got some savings. More than my shares in the company. I'll cut my salary down to just enough to cover my health insurance."

"You can't do that."

"I'm in charge of payroll. Be pretty hard to stop me. And, I can just about guarantee that everybody else would understand a cut in pay. In fact, they would support the idea, so we don't have to close."

"No. Let's take it slow. Holidays are just about here. I'm not taking Christmas dinner out of any mouths."

"You're a good man, Evan." Perry sighed. "I'm just not sure you know when to say no."

Chapter Three

"No!" Evan looked exasperated as he spoke to his father.

Gordon put his hand on Jimmy's shoulder. "If you don't have time now to show Jimmy the quarry, we'll do it another day."

Chloe held her breath, hoping the men wouldn't argue.

"Course I could do it myself..." Gordon continued. "Not sure I still have my keys to the outer gates, though."

Evan rolled his eyes heavenward. "I'll fit it in this week or next. Don't you have enough to keep busy today?"

Gordon rubbed his chin in thought. "Well, I do have a doctor's appointment...."

Chloe choked back unexpected laughter, coughing to cover the sound. Gordon had told them he had a checkup scheduled with the foot doctor. He sure was milking the excuse for all it was worth. And clearly it was working.

Concern filled Evan's face. "You didn't tell me."

Gordon shrugged, his face on the verge of woeful. "You've already got a lot on your mind."

Evan glanced at his father, then plunked a pile of papers down on his desk. "You want me to take you to the doctor?"

Clearing his throat, Gordon shook his head. "Not necessary."

Reluctantly, Evan shifted his gaze to Chloe. "I'll show them around the quarry. But I can't spend all day."

Chloe knew his last words were directed at her. "I've never been to a quarry before."

"I've never met any women who wanted to before."

Tension bubbled through the air like hail stones.

"So that's settled." Gordon turned to leave. "I'll see you all back at the house."

"I told you I can't…" Evan didn't bother to complete the sentence since his father was walking away without listening.

"Spend all day," Chloe completed for him. "Jimmy and I understand, don't we, big guy?"

Jimmy, looking intimidated by Evan, nodded tentatively.

For the briefest moment, Evan's countenance turned utterly bleak. He shook the expression off as quickly as it had formed, then picked up his phone, punching in a few numbers. "Perry? Push the meeting with Alsom back two hours." He listened a few moments. "Oh yeah, I'll definitely be back in time for the bank."

Chloe got the message. The visit would be brief, but any time Evan spent with Jimmy would help.

Outside, parked in front of the building, were a few shiny new SUVs and three double-cab trucks. At the end of the row was a beat-up pickup truck. Since all of the vehicles were emblazoned with Mitchell Stone logos, Chloe trailed behind Evan waiting to hear the chirp of doors unlocking.

When he paused in front of the ragged old beater, Chloe couldn't help staring.

Evan walked to the passenger door and opened it.

Jimmy immediately tugged on her hand. "You get in first, please?"

Since he drew out *please* like a deathbed request, she reluctantly scooted over to the middle position in the single cab.

While Evan slid in front of the steering wheel, Chloe scrunched over as close as possible to Jimmy.

Glancing in the rearview mirror, Evan backed out on to the lazy Main Street. Even though it was near noon, not much traffic flowed through the quaint downtown area that looked as though it had stayed primarily the same since Victorian times.

"Swell truck," she commented.

He darted a glance, obviously gauging her sarcasm. "It was my grandfather's."

"It's nice."

The corners of his mouth curled down.

"That you kept it, I mean," she added hastily. "A lot of people just want the newest model. I think sentiment's more important."

"Hmm."

Chloe had already figured out that he wouldn't be easily convinced of anything. Apparently, Evan was equally economic with his words.

As they rolled out of town toward the quarry, the old truck bumped considerably. One especially large bump thrust her against Evan's shoulder. Feeling as though she had hit heated rock, Chloe drew back, immediately scooting toward the passenger-side door.

"Ouch," Jimmy squeaked.

"I'm sorry! I was…concentrating too much on the landscape." At the moment she couldn't have guessed if they were surrounded by mountains or desert.

"You mean the trees?"

Feeling smaller than the child at her side, she tried to look unaffected. "Pretty aren't they?"

Actually they were. Leaves had transformed into clusters of color. Standing next to sentinel green pines, this was the beautiful Texas hill country she'd heard so much about. But the squiggle in her stomach didn't have anything to do with the surroundings—the nonhuman ones, that was. Still feeling the impression of Evan's shoulder against her arm, she wanted to touch the spot, to see if the fire she'd felt was external. Ridiculous, she knew. A grown woman practically melting by the accidental brush of a man's arm. A very handsome man's arm.

"We're not far," Evan announced.

Still ruminating on her reaction, again she over-reacted, jumping when he spoke. "Well... that's good then." At this rate she would reduce her conversational skills to a first grader's level.

"Look!" Jimmy poked her as his voice threaded with something close to excitement.

Chloe followed his gaze. A beautiful horse trotted in a field, lifting its head in a royal motion.

Evan didn't take his eyes from the road. "He's an Arabian. Belongs to the Markhams."

"That's a neat trick," she commented. "How did you know without looking?"

"This is my home," he explained simply.

"Still...."

"At the curve, there's an old oak that's got more notches on it than an outlaw's gun. One of them's mine. Most everybody in town's hit that oak when they were learning to drive. Luckily, the tree's over far enough that no one's run into it straight on."

How could a man who obviously cared about his home and employees have absolutely no compassion for a parentless child? Burdened with the thought, Chloe didn't ask any more questions as Evan drove farther from town. Jimmy, still intimidated, didn't speak either. And Evan clearly wasn't going to initiate a conversation.

In the quiet, Chloe saw much more of the gently rolling hills, the yellowing of wild grass, the last wildflowers struggling to survive despite the bite of late autumn. The hill country really was a beautiful place for the holidays.

Back home, they would have a wintry cold Thanksgiving and a guaranteed white Christmas. She wasn't missing the weather. Or her job. Just her mother. And Barbara Reed had been insistent that Chloe accept this assignment. Still, she was so used to caring for her mother…visiting her in the long-term recovery facility, spending every spare minute with her. Intensely aware of the thousand-plus miles that separated them, Chloe sighed.

"Something wrong?" Evan asked.

Again, his unexpected speaking startled her. This time her hand flew to her throat to disguise the rapid pulse that must be visible. "No… of course not."

"Hmm."

How did the man run a business when he barely spoke? Feeling the opportunity, she cleared her throat. "Actually, I was thinking about my mother. Missing her."

Evan took his eyes from the road. "Then why'd you come all the way out here?"

Because she needed the money Mr. Wainwright had offered to continue paying for her mother's care.

Jimmy looked up at her and she smiled for his benefit. "I wouldn't miss this adventure for anything."

Evan snorted. "Adventure?"

"Sure, neither of us has ever been to Texas." Chloe struggled for something benign to say. "Or a quarry."

This time when he glanced at her, she met his dark eyes, sustaining the gaze. Despite the disbelief lurking in their depths, she felt the same as she had when she'd bumped into his shoulder. Silly but....

Chloe swallowed. She hadn't experienced that kind of reaction to a man since her ex-fiancé, Derek, had dumped her. Must just be nerves, she told herself. That, and knowing how much was riding on her swaying Evan Mitchell to change his mind.

Still, she straightened up, holding her body rigidly in place. And kept herself in that position until they neared a large sign indicating the quarry. Unexpectedly excited, Chloe leaned forward when Evan turned off the main road.

Bumping over the rutted dirt road, dust billowed behind them in a dark cloud. Evan didn't slow down. Clearly the pitted road was familiar to him, so familiar he knew its ups and downs, its twists and curves.

Not surprisingly, the small office, barely more than a shed, was built of limestone.

"Is the quarry in that building?" Jimmy asked in a disappointed voice.

Evan chuckled, startling Chloe and Jimmy. "Nope. It's the big pit we're driving to when we switch vehicles."

Transfixed by the difference in Evan when he smiled, Chloe didn't pay attention to the quarry until Jimmy poked her arm, pointing out the large slabs of stone literally everywhere.

Chloe tried to think of something intelligent to say; she reverted to the familiar. "Do you sell stone from this office?"

"Small jobs like home remodels. All the commercial orders come through the main office." He pulled the truck up close to the small building.

"Is the quarry nearby?" Chloe asked, as curious as Jimmy.

"We'll grab a buggy to get over there." Evan got out of the truck and disappeared.

Chloe wriggled her eyebrows at Jimmy. "Sounds cool."

He loosened up slightly. "Evan doesn't even sound mad at me."

Chloe's heart pinged and she impulsively wrapped

her arms around him. "He isn't mad at you, honey. If anything, he's mad at himself."

"How come?"

Yes. Why? "Because he's the sort of man who's used to being in control, in charge, like at his company. And, when Evan's in unfamiliar territory...he's confused. And that makes him mad. Let's get out of the truck and be ready when he brings the buggy around, okay?"

Evan appeared shortly in what resembled a golf cart. "Hop in."

When Jimmy hesitated, Chloe climbed in, taking a spot in the back so Jimmy could ride up front next to Evan.

When Jimmy continued to hesitate, Evan's impatient expression relented a fraction; he shrugged his head to one side. "Come on. You ride shotgun."

Once Jimmy was onboard, Evan didn't speed off as Chloe imagined he wanted to. Instead, he drove slowly, pointing out various formations.

"This quarry is limestone." Evan pointed to a newly excavated vein. "See the different colors? The clay and the iron oxide cause that." He drove past the open pit to a second pit. "Now, this limestone's been weathered a long time, about a hundred and forty years. That's why the color's different than the new vein. Subtle change, though. Takes stone thousands of years to form, sometimes more to change."

Jimmy's big brown eyes grew even larger. "How do you grow more, then?"

Evan's mouth curved as though about to smile. As quickly, he pulled his eyebrows together in a serious expression. "We can't. Have you heard about taking care of the environment?"

Solemnly, Jimmy nodded. "Daddy and Mommy said we have to take care of the earth. That it's our job, so that's why we have to use green things." He looked up at Evan. "That doesn't mean the color green."

"So I've heard. Which is why we use every part of the stone we dig up. After the big slabs are cut, we use the small pieces for all kinds of things—cement, mortar, it even goes in toothpaste."

"We brush our teeth with rocks?" Jimmy asked, forgetting his fear, completely intrigued.

Evan's lips definitely twitched. "Helps that they flavor it with mint. Oh, and bubble gum for kids."

Bubble-gum flavored toothpaste? Funny thing for a single man to know about. Mr. Wainwright had told her that Evan was an only child. So no nieces or nephews. Of course he could have seen the product in a commercial.

Chloe had wondered if Evan's stubborn refusal to even consider taking Jimmy in was because of being an only child. Never having to share. Maybe he hadn't left the trait behind with his childhood. Maybe he didn't want to share his life, either.

She found that terribly sad. Even though Chloe had felt the impact of financial problems for years, she wouldn't trade caring for her mother. Not for a zillion dollars. But the money Holden Wainwright had promised her if she succeeded in placing Jimmy with the Mitchells would change their lives. There would be no more angst-ridden moments of worrying whether she would be able to pay the rising costs of the care facility.

"Are most of the rocks for toothpaste?" Jimmy was asking Evan.

"Nope. Most of it's used in architecture. Have you heard of the Great Pyramids? They're in Egypt where your grandparents are. Anyway, they're made of limestone."

"I didn't know that," Chloe blurted out, belatedly realizing she had verbalized her thought.

"Castles in medieval times were made from it, too." Evan replied, unperturbed by her question.

"With dragons?" Jimmy asked with the first note of genuine, full-out excitement she had heard in his voice.

Evan scratched his head. "Hard to say. We don't carry dragons at our quarries."

Chloe nearly giggled aloud, not something she would have ever anticipated doing with Evan.

The thought had barely formed when he turned around. "I have to get back to the office soon. Where did you leave your car?"

"The house," she admitted, belatedly realizing that hadn't been a well-thought-out plan.

Evan glanced at his watch, then scowled. "Have to head back now, then."

By the time they returned the cart and switched back to the truck, Evan was impatient to get to his meeting. He pulled into the driveway at the house, leaving the engine running. Jimmy hopped out immediately. Chloe started to follow, but Evan caught her arm.

"We have to talk. Soon." He met her eyes, his own making her shiver unexpectedly. "When we're alone."

Chapter Four

Alone. Evan waited through dinner, then coffee and cake in the parlor. Chloe had managed to keep someone within a foot of her the entire time. He wouldn't be surprised if she super-glued Jimmy to one of her hands.

And his head was throbbing. The meeting with the bank president had gone so poorly he didn't expect a follow-up visit would change a thing. Evan, like the rest of his family before him, had kept his business with the local bank. No connections to any of the large multinational banks. He couldn't blame his local banker. Loans, especially big commercial loans, still weren't the flavor of the day. And Mitchell Stone had been operating in the red for the last three years.

It hadn't helped that during the meeting, he couldn't forget his other immediate problem. Sending Chloe and Jimmy back to Milwaukee. The boy resembled Spencer too much, making him remember too much…about too many things.

A sudden image of Sean seared his thoughts. His son would be seven now, too. Sean should have been the one sitting in the cart beside him as they toured the quarry, learning as Evan had, from a young age to appreciate both the family business and the blessings of the earth, what it gave up to us.

Sean had wanted to learn—every waking moment of every day. What kind of bird nested in the tall oak out front? Why did Grandpa's hair turn gray? How did the dew form on the grass? A million questions, he had thought at the time, hoping he wouldn't run out of answers. He had never dreamed it would be Sean who would run out of time.

And his beautiful Robin… The Lord had never made a sweeter woman. She had lived her life for her family, and ultimately died trying to save Sean. If only…. If only he hadn't chosen Hawaii to vacation. But Robin had always wanted to visit there and he had delighted at the surprise on her face when he had given her a dream vacation for her birthday. She and Sean had counted the days until they flew to the beautiful islands.

Evan would give anything to turn back the calendar, to change that one dreadful decision. He swallowed, knowing life didn't work that way.

"Son?" Gordon repeated.

Evan shook his head, then lifted his gaze. "Sorry, Dad."

Gordon's eyes filled with empathy and understanding. "I'm going to teach Jimmy how to tie some flies. Thought we'd go fishing Saturday. How does that sound?"

Like another painful reminder. "Whatever you want."

Concern lingered in Gordon's eyes.

And Evan didn't want to worry his father. "Be good to go before winter sets in." Thanksgiving was right around the corner; Christmas would descend in seeming days.

"That's what I was thinking. Chloe says her father used to go ice fishing up in Wisconsin. Makes my bones shiver to think about it."

Evan glanced in her direction. "Doesn't your father ice fish anymore?"

"My dad died when I was in junior high school," she explained. Although Chloe's voice was steady, he glimpsed a flash of pain in her eyes.

"Sorry." Evan knew the words were inadequate. He had heard the phrase often enough in the past two years.

"It's been a long time."

But never long enough. Time heals all wounds. He had heard that one so much it made him sick. That and *the Lord never gives us more than we can bear.* But there had been no reason to take Robin and Sean. Again his throat swelled and Evan couldn't speak around the lump it caused.

Chloe glanced down, then patted Jimmy's knee. Clearly, she knew that the discussion could upset him, might have already done so.

Evan wondered how Wainwright had found this woman. Someone as pugnacious as a bulldog, yet obviously sensitive to a child's needs.

Gordon stood and clapped one hand on Jimmy's shoulder. "Let's go in the den. Those flies aren't going to tie themselves."

They had barely begun walking from the room when Chloe rose. When she passed his chair, Evan snagged her arm.

Startled, Chloe pulled back, her hand immediately brushing the spot where he had touched her.

Funny, he felt a strange tingle at the touch himself. Ignoring it, Evan waited until Gordon and Jimmy were out of hearing. "We need to talk."

"In here?" she asked weakly.

"No. Too many interruptions." He stood, grabbing her hand. Again the feeling shot clear through his body. Again he ignored it. He led her through the kitchen, out the back door. The wide, wrap-around porch was lit by soft gas lights.

"The days are shorter," Chloe commented, sounding nervous. "Gets dark so early." She pointed toward the sky. "Good there's moonlight."

"Are you a stargazer, Miss Reed?"

"Chloe," she insisted. "Yes, I suppose I am. Not that I've had time to—"

"How *do* you spend your time? Convincing people to make bad decisions?"

Anger flashed in her sea-green eyes. She was right. The light from the moon aided the gas lights enough to read her expression. Chloe's mouth opened, then she firmed her lips into a resolute line as she pulled her shoulders back. "I work, if you must know."

"That's what you call it?"

The anger in her face intensified. "What did you want to talk to me about?"

So, she had a temper. "Surely it's clear, even to you, that Wainwright's plan isn't going to work."

"Why are you so negative? You act as though Jimmy has some sort of disease. He's a wonderful child!"

"I didn't say he isn't." The boy seemed like a good kid. On the quiet side, but Evan didn't expect anything different after what Jimmy had been through.

"Then what is it?" Exasperation spilled into her voice.

"I told you my answer is *no*."

Chloe paused, tilting her face so that the moonlight enhanced the beguiling heart shape of her face. "Your father seems to have a different opinion."

Evan tried to ignore the unwanted feeling her

proximity caused. "It's not going to work, regardless of what my father says. There's no room in my life for a child. I'm fighting to keep the business alive. I have twenty-seven employees who depend on me for their livelihood. Do you expect me to forget about them?"

"Of course not." The exasperation had left her voice. Concern replaced it. "But that doesn't mean you can't do both. You have help—your father, Thelma and Ned."

"What is it about *no* that you don't understand? This isn't like a pet rescue. I can't turn Jimmy out in the yard with Bailey if I don't want him close to me. He needs parents, not a guardian."

"But with time—"

"There isn't going to be any time." Evan's constant anguish flared so fiercely it felt like a physical blow. The back door opened and Jimmy ran outside, followed more slowly by Gordon.

"Guess what?" Jimmy asked Chloe with a glimmer of excitement. "Tomorrow we're going to see the school."

All four adults looked at one another. Chloe seemed uncertain. Gordon was determined. And Evan knew he had to stop this from happening. At all costs.

Chloe and Jimmy had disappeared upstairs. Evan made certain of it before he confronted his father.

"What were you thinking? Telling the boy you'll show him our school?"

Gordon knocked the ashes from his pipe into an ashtray. "Why shouldn't he see it?"

"You know exactly why. Jimmy will think that means he'll be staying on for a while."

"Son, he needs us."

Evan snorted. "There are thousands of orphaned children who need homes. Are we going to take them in as well?"

Gordon packed cherry tobacco into the bowl of his worn pipe. "He's family."

Evan felt his chest heave with pain. Family would never again mean the same thing for him. "Are you planning to take care of him?"

"We had that talk when Wainwright first called."

Slumping into a deep leather chair, Evan sighed. "Why are you doing this to me, Dad?"

Gordon stopped tamping down the tobacco, which didn't really matter since he never lit the pipe. "It's not *to* you, son. It's *for* you. When we first lost Robin and Sean, I knew it would take you a long time to accept that you still have a life. It's natural."

"*Accept* it? I'll never accept it. There was no reason for them to die."

"You did everything you could to—"

"But the Lord didn't!" Furious, he rose.

"We don't always understand—"

"I've heard it all before. And I don't want to hear it again."

Gordon sighed. "This boy is another chance for you, son. The Lord knows of the hole in your heart."

"A replacement?" Evan laughed bitterly. "A cosmic reparation? No. I lost the only son I'll ever have."

"Evan, you—"

"If you persist in having them stay here, he's your responsibility."

"Son, it doesn't do you any good to be angry at the Lord."

Sadness and pain settled in Evan's heart. "I'm not angry at Him. I'm disappointed. And that won't ever change."

"All the grades go together?" Jimmy asked in a hushed voice, tightening his grip on Chloe's hand as they stood in the main hall of Rosewood Community Church's school.

"Not in the same room," Chloe explained, although she wasn't certain just how the school was organized.

Gordon nodded. "That's how it was when I was a boy."

Jimmy looked at him in awe, as though the older man had said he had attended school with the dinosaurs. "*You* went to school here?"

Chloe and Gordon both chuckled.

"Yep. We'd invented fire by then." Gordon clapped one hand on Jimmy's shoulder, giving him a small hug while he exchanged an amused glance with Chloe.

Just then a pretty woman walked out of the office.

"Well, hello, Grace."

"Gordon!" She smiled, a generous smile that lit up her blue-gray eyes. "I heard the hunting went very well."

He turned to Chloe. "Ah, the bane of small towns. Can't get by with much that everybody doesn't know about."

"Afraid that's true," Grace agreed.

"I'm forgetting my manners. Grace, this is Chloe Reed and Jimmy Mitchell."

"So good to meet you," she said to Chloe, then extended her hand to Jimmy. "Always glad to meet another Mitchell man."

Pleased, but shy, Jimmy grinned.

"I don't have a class this hour," Grace continued. "Can I help you find anything?"

"Thought it'd be nice to show them around. You know, a little tour, before they meet the principal," Gordon explained.

"I'd be glad to help. I teach part-time in the upper grades, but I know all the buildings." She leaned down slightly toward Jimmy and confided, "The kids call me *old lady Brady*."

Chloe couldn't restrain her laughter. "We're probably close in age. Didn't realize I was in that category yet."

Grace laughed with her. "Came as quite a shock to me, too. Teaching is my second and best career. Didn't realize it would age me so!"

Gordon groaned. "You kids are killing me."

"You are a sweetheart," Grace declared as she turned to Chloe. "See why I love the Mitchell men?"

Chloe had seen plenty of reasons, even in Evan. Because for all his protests, she suspected he was covering a deep and grievous hurt.

Grace led them down the main hall. "We're in the administration building. Besides the office, the cafeteria, library and auditorium are in this building. There are separate buildings for elementary, junior high and senior high. Since it's a church school, we're not funded by the government but we have private donors. I imagine you'd like to see the elementary building."

The cheerful building was filled with colorful banners and posters. "Kindergarten through fifth-grade classes," Grace explained as they passed individual classrooms. "There's also a smaller, all-purpose room for the youngest grades. The plays and larger performances are held in the auditorium. More room for all the doting parents and grandparents." Grace paused in front of one classroom. "This is a first-grade class."

"Is there more than one?" Chloe asked, liking the positive energy in the school.

"That depends on enrollment. Our elementary teachers are certified to teach two or three grades. That way we can adjust to make sure class sizes aren't too large."

"Sounds like you've thought of everything."

"Are you a teacher, too?" Grace questioned.

"No. I'm a sec... I work for a legal firm out of Milwaukee."

Gordon looked at her strangely, and Chloe fiddled with her purse handles, worrying about her near slip.

"A fellow big-city native! I'm from Houston."

Chloe was immediately curious. "How do you like living here?"

"It's perfect," she replied in a soft voice. "I love it."

"Met her husband here," Gordon added.

Grace blushed, a gentle pink. "Yes. You'll meet him at church. He's the choir director."

"A musician?"

She smiled widely. "Actually, Noah's a plastic surgeon who happens to love music. Works out well because I do, too."

"Do you teach music?"

"Actually, I teach English." Grace laughed again.

"You probably think you've wandered into the land of Oz where nothing is as it seems. A choir director who's a doctor and a musician who teaches English."

Chloe liked Grace's infectious smile and laughter. "I'm enjoying Oz just fine."

"Are we in Oz?" Jimmy asked in a confused tone.

Chloe met Grace's glance and broke into another round of laughter. Then she knelt down next to Jimmy. "Oz is a pretend place. It's very colorful and full of surprises."

With a child's understanding, Jimmy nodded. "But the school's real?"

"Very," Gordon replied. "Do you like what you've seen?"

Jimmy nodded. "I don't like big schools."

"Me, either," Grace confided. "I was kind of scared when I started teaching, but at this school, all the people are nice and welcoming. In no time, I felt right at home."

Grace might teach upper grades, but she had the perfect touch for young children. Chloe was glad they had run into her. She mouthed *thank you* above Jimmy's head.

"I know how it is to be new to Rosewood," Grace continued. She reached into her pocket, pulling out a pen and notepad. She scribbled on one page quickly, then handed it to Chloe. "This is my cell number. I'd like to help you settle in."

Chloe felt at a loss as to how to answer. Her position was so tenuous.

Gordon replied for her. "That's mighty nice of you, Grace. And, of course, we'll see you at church Sunday."

Church. Because she spent every Sunday visiting her mother, it had been a long time since Chloe had been in a church. But their pastor visited at the care facility, mostly seeing her mom. Chloe's faith had never wavered. Which was comforting, because she would need it now more than ever.

Chapter Five

Evan could scarcely believe he had been dragged into this fishing trip. With mountains of work waiting on his desk, he was standing on the shore of the river, casting into the flowing currents. He glanced over at his father. After breakfast, as the others were readying for the trip, his father had sat down suddenly, seeming out of breath. Gordon insisted he was all right. So much so that it worried Evan. Was it a ruse to make him go fishing as well? To spend more time with Jimmy?

His father refused to call the doctor or stop by the clinic, which was open Saturday mornings. Ruse or not, Evan couldn't let him drive out to the river with only Chloe and Jimmy. She didn't know the area. If something happened, they could be stuck, far from help.

Gordon's last checkup had gone well, but he wasn't a young man anymore. The thought chilled him. Once his father was gone, Evan would be the only one left. Feeling his gaze pulled as though by a strong magnet, Evan looked at young Jimmy. The only one left in his family.

Why had Spencer and his wife insisted on reopening that abandoned factory? Wainwright had told Evan that the newly refurbished machines ran on clean energy, apparently a fervent cause of Spencer's. And, he intended to employ people who had been jobless through no fault of their own. It was a noble cause. But the cost?

Bailey nudged his muzzle into Evan's hand. Absently, he petted the golden's head. Next to the shore, Jimmy stood between Chloe and Gordon. The boy had taken a shine to Gordon. But then Jimmy hadn't really had a grandparent relationship before. His maternal grandfather had died when Jimmy was a toddler, that grandmother suffered from late-stage Alzheimer's.

And, Evan wondered if the child had ever even met his paternal grandparents. Obviously, Spencer's parents hadn't changed since Spencer was a child. Devoted to their archeological dig, they had tunnel vision when it came to anything else in life. He supposed they loved Spencer in their own way. But they had seen nothing wrong in letting him grow up virtually alone. When Evan was young, he had overheard his parents disparaging over why they had ever had a child since they didn't seem to want to be parents.

His gaze roved toward Chloe. He had expected her to be a typical city woman, squeamish and ill at ease. Instead, she eagerly baited Jimmy's hook and now stood next to the hill country river as though she'd done so a hundred times before. In the sunlight, her long hair gleamed like spun honey. And Chloe's laughter was easy and often. Yet she still wore her mother-bear persona, keeping Jimmy under her watchful eye.

Only a week and a half before Thanksgiving, the mild hill country weather was holding true. The changing leaves proved autumn had arrived, but the bite of winter wasn't yet in the wind. It wouldn't be long though, bringing the holidays he now dreaded.

As Evan watched, his father sat down in his camp chair, something he usually didn't do until he had fished for several hours. They'd only been at the river about two hours. Although Gordon's fishing rod still rested in the river, he wasn't casting it any longer.

Frowning, Evan studied his face. The niggling worry resurfaced. He walked casually over to Gordon's side. "River's running low. Probably won't catch much today."

Gordon nodded toward Jimmy. "Never know."

Clearly, his father wanted Jimmy to have a good time and Evan knew better than to suggest they go home early. His father would dig his feet in and not budge. But if he helped Jimmy catch a fish…

Sighing, Evan reached for the thermos, poured a hot cup of coffee and handed it to his father.

"Thanks, son." Gordon's voice sounded weary.

There was a second thermos with hot cocoa for Jimmy, but the youngster was so absorbed in the new sport that Evan could tell he didn't care about refreshments at the moment. Manners drilled in by a determined mother couldn't be ignored. "Chloe? Coffee?"

Chloe turned, her mouth wide with a smile, sunshine illuminating her face. "Thanks, no." Their gazes still connected, she hesitated for a moment before turning back to the river.

It was a terminally long moment, yet not nearly long enough.

Evan frowned, then shook his head. Trick of the light, he decided. Nothing more.

Yet he continued to watch as she gracefully arched her back as she prepared to cast her line into the river. It plopped into the water perfectly. *She must have gone fly fishing with her father as well as ice fishing.* It took time to learn to cast like that. Which was why they'd given Jimmy a pole instead. Although the boy had helped tie flies, he was still too young to master casting. Maybe in the spring when there was plenty of warm weather ahead…. Evan jerked his thoughts to an abrupt halt. No. Jimmy wouldn't be here in the spring.

Reminded that the boy needed to catch a fish so they

could get his father back home, Evan paused. His own gear lay in the yellowing grass. He had brought it along only to appease his father. But it gave him an excuse to help Jimmy.

Evan walked to the shore quietly so he wouldn't startle the boy. Studying his wobbling line, Evan remembered his own father teaching him to fish. Then he remembered the times he had brought Sean to this very shore, the bubbling excitement of his son's animated face. Evan had expected someday to be the one sitting in a camp chair while Sean taught his own child the sport.

Evan felt a light tug on his arm and looked down.

Jimmy's upturned face was quizzical. "Do you want to use my fishing rod?"

A sweet gesture. Evan swallowed and pushed away the emotion. "Thought maybe I could watch awhile. You using worms or minnows?"

"Uncle Gordon said I could use his best fly, but Chloe said I'd better start with worms."

Uncle Gordon? Evan pushed past the moniker. "That's how I began. Takes a while to learn how to cast."

"Like Chloe and Uncle Gordon?"

"Yep."

"Uncle Gordon must be a neat dad."

The remark caught him completely off guard. "You had a pretty neat dad yourself."

Pain flooded Jimmy's eyes. "We were going to go on a boat next summer. Mommy, too."

Chloe met Evan's gaze over the boy's head.

She knelt down so she was at the child's level. "They would be so proud of you. How you've been so brave about starting a new school. And now, learning a new sport!" Chloe's clear green eyes beamed with empathy and Jimmy's expression started to clear.

Paralyzed with shared grief, Evan couldn't speak. But there was no condemnation in Chloe's eyes. It was almost as though she understood what he was going through. But that couldn't be.

Gathering his senses, Evan watched quietly for a while. When Jimmy's line snagged, Evan could tell it wasn't a fish. "Looks like you're caught up in some brush."

Jimmy frowned, then tugged on the rod, but it didn't yield.

"This is the good part of fishing with bait. No big deal to lose a worm, but when you lose your favorite fly…."

"Oh." Jimmy's eyes widened. "I'm glad I didn't lose the fly."

He was so serious that Evan wanted to pat his shoulder, tell the boy to relax. Instead, he cut the line and reached in the tackle box for a small hook and bobber.

"Is it bad to lose a hook?" Jimmy asked in a near whisper.

Evan couldn't stop his smile. "Nope. That's part of fishing—the worms, hooks and line. We don't waste them on purpose, but it's not bad when we lose some."

Jimmy visibly exhaled.

"What do you want to use for bait this time?" They had stopped by the bait shack and picked up leeches, worms and minnows.

Jimmy shrugged his narrow shoulders, his eyes still anxious. "Which one should we pick?"

"In the spring, you can find all the earthworms you need right in the yard. I used to collect them to sell to the bait store. Don't suppose kids do that anymore."

"They don't?" Jimmy's expression remained sober.

Evan knew the child shouldn't have to always be so cautious and serious. "Let's try a minnow this time, okay?"

"Okay."

Evan showed him how to slip the tiny fish on to the end of the hook. Jimmy's small hands were practically hidden under his while the youngster tried to imitate the process. "Go ahead and drop your line in the water."

Jimmy obliged, watching eagerly as the sinker took the bait under the surface. "Will the big fishes see the little one?"

"They see your bait move. They're attracted to

the colors, too. That's why fly fishers spend so much time making their lures."

"We used feathers," Jimmy confided. "Yellow ones."

Gordon made an art of tying flies. Evan hid a smile as he imagined the ones the pair had created. Glancing to his other side, he watched Chloe whisk her fly into the air, then back over her shoulder, finally casting it forward in a perfect motion. "You've had a lot of practice."

"My father was an avid fisherman. We learned how to tie a fly about the same time we learned how to tie our shoes."

"Big family?"

"One brother. Chip and his family are stationed in Germany."

"Your mother?"

Chloe looked straight ahead, not meeting his gaze. "Mom lives in an extended-care facility."

He frowned, wondering at this aspect. "She's ill?"

"COPD. It's a chronic pulmonary disease. She has to be on oxygen, among other things. So she can't safely live on her own. If she were to lose consciousness while she's alone…" Chloe glanced down at Jimmy who was concentrating on the bobber on his fishing line. "Fortunately, she's surrounded by people."

"Allows you to have a life of your own."

Chloe's head jerked sideways as though it, too, were connected to a string. Indignation was written on every feature. "You really believe that?"

"Isn't that why people use nursing homes?" He wasn't sure why she was so indignant. She was more than a thousand miles from Milwaukee.

"It's *not* a nursing home." Seeing that Jimmy was staring at her, Chloe quieted her voice. "My mother's living where she's safe. Not all of us have the means to stay home and employ others so that our loved ones have constant care."

Evan caught the barb in her words, but still didn't understand her injured expression. He certainly hadn't asked her to cross the country, leaving her mother behind. In fact, he couldn't understand why she had. Especially when she was prepared to dig in and stay as long as it took for him to give in about Jimmy. And all the while her mother was left on her own. Cold-blooded, Evan decided. To choose whatever amount of money Wainwright was offering over the welfare of her mother.

The chill of Evan's words superceded the late autumn weather. Chloe could scarcely believe his accusation. She had sacrificed everything to care for her mother. Working as a legal secretary barely covered the cost of the extended-care facility. As the rates continued to rise, Chloe despaired about how she would be able to afford it. For herself, she lived in a cheap one-room, efficiency apartment. Not that it mattered. She spent all her weekends visiting with Mom. And days at the law firm were long. Since Chloe's fiancé had dumped her, she had virtually no social life. Derek couldn't understand her devotion to family and Chloe couldn't understand how she could have been so wrong about him.

When Mr. Wainwright offered to pay her way through law school, along with a full salary, Chloe couldn't turn down his proposition. As an attorney, she would be better prepared to afford a lifetime of payments to the care facility. And, she had promised herself she would never put her mother, Barbara, in a state facility. Her younger brother's military pay was barely enough to support his growing family. Besides, Chloe had promised her father she would look out for the others.

All she had to do was happily settle Jimmy in with Evan Mitchell. It would probably be easier to push a rock across the country with her nose. She hadn't imagined anyone could turn away a child like Jimmy. Even though Derek had proven to be the wrong choice, Chloe longed for the family she had dreamed of having with him. She was twenty-seven years old. Much longer and her biological clock would run out of batteries.

Trying not to be obvious, she checked on Jimmy. He was watching Evan's every move, trying to imitate the tall man's every motion. Bailey's plumed tail thumped happily against Evan's endlessly long legs.

Keeping her eyelids down, Chloe tried to hide her interest. Clad in jeans, boots and a casual Western shirt, Evan cut an impressive figure. Not many men in the city could have pulled off the look. And there was something about the rugged image that had always intrigued her. True, she had often been in the Wisconsin countryside where plenty of men wore jeans. But not quite the way Evan did.

Chloe's fishing line jerked suddenly. Having relaxed her grip while stargazing, the rod slipped right through her hands. She hadn't done anything so amateurish since she was a kid.

Evan reacted before she could, reaching a long arm toward her escaping fishing gear. Chloe found herself duplicating Jimmy's reaction as they both stared, open-mouthed at him.

"Got it." Evan turned back, holding the fishing rod, water dripping from his strong fingers.

And Chloe swallowed, unable to think of a single word to say. Realizing her mouth must be practically flapping open, she snapped her lips shut.

"That was neat!" Jimmy declared, impressed.

"Yes...." Chloe cleared her throat. "Thank you. I don't know what I was thinking." But she could tell what Evan was thinking. That she surely *hadn't* been thinking.

He handed her the rescued rod. "No problem."

Right. It wasn't even her own gear she had almost lost.

Gordon waved to her from his chair. "Don't worry, Chloe. It's just a fishing rod."

One of his favorites. He'd told her so when he had insisted she use it that day.

Chloe met Evan's startled gaze. His eyes narrowed.

That wasn't a good sign.

When Evan spoke, she nearly dropped the pole again. "Better keep a good grip on what you don't want to lose."

She swallowed. "Right."

"Let's check your bait," Evan said, turning to Jimmy.

While he helped the boy put fresh bait on the hook, Chloe suddenly felt a million miles from home. Was she crazy for accepting this assignment? The holidays were around the corner. Even though Mom had insisted she would be surrounded by friends at the care facility, Chloe hated the thought of not being there for her.

Jimmy plunked his freshly baited line back in the water just as Evan instructed. Only moments later his float bobbed, then disappeared beneath the water's surface.

"A fish!" Knowing not to, Chloe didn't raise her

voice. But inside she was shouting. Jimmy needed a victory. Even one as minor as catching his first fish.

"You've got him," Evan encouraged.

Jimmy's hands shook as he hung on to the pole.

Evan moved behind him, reaching forward to grasp Jimmy's hands, adding his strength.

The fish flopped as together, they reeled him in. Shades of silver glinted in the sunlight while Evan dipped the net beneath the struggling fish.

"Wow," Jimmy breathed. "We really caught it."

"You did," Evan amended. "I just helped. Now we have to decide what to do with him. No one else has caught anything. And, big as he is, this guy isn't enough to feed everyone. So, do you want to keep him or let him go back in the water?"

Jimmy pinched his lips together in concentration. "He probably wants to go back."

"Good decision." Evan removed the unbarbed single hook from the fish's jaw and quickly tossed it back in the river. The frantic creature wiggled and dove before swimming away. "They have to get back in to the water real fast to survive."

"Will he be okay?" Jimmy asked, staring where the fish had disappeared.

"Looks like it. Good job."

Chloe stared at Evan, wondering if the man had any idea of how good he was with Jimmy. He was a natural. And, if Evan wasn't so stubborn, he would at least *consider* accepting guardianship. Instead, he acted like an old man set in his ways. Well, that wasn't exactly true. Gordon had welcomed Jimmy with open arms. What could have slammed Evan's mind completely shut?

Chapter Six

With Thanksgiving only days away, Chloe was torn. Even though Jimmy had begun shadowing Evan whenever he was home, she still had no idea whether Evan would change his mind.

Sitting in the den with her cup of hot tea, she watched Jimmy through the large window. He was running and playing with Bailey, the dog eager to fetch and retrieve endlessly. If Evan had been home, both boy and dog would be tagging behind him. And Evan would still be telling her that Jimmy's attention wasn't going to change his mind. Overcome with indecision, she sighed.

"That's a mighty big sigh for a little lady," Gordon commented as he entered the room.

She turned. "Sorry. Just thinking."

"No need to apologize for your thoughts. Sounds like you have plenty on your mind."

Chloe met his kind eyes. "I'm trying to decide

whether I should take Jimmy back to Milwaukee before he gets too attached."

Gordon took his time to settle into a deep leather chair. The aged cowhide was as supple as a lambskin glove. "You know, I've lived in this house, in this town, all my life. I met my wife here. Raised my son. Buried my parents, my brother." He paused. "More people than I want to count. Retired from my business because it was time…because it was Evan's turn. He's done well by the quarry. I wouldn't have wanted to be in his shoes with the economy these past years." Gordon glanced down, quiet for a few moments. "He doesn't ask, my son. He tells. But I ask because I've learned sometimes it's the best thing a person can do. I asked the Lord to give Evan some peace…happiness. And He sent you. You and Jimmy."

Chloe didn't speak, overcome by the emotion in Gordon's words, wondering what he meant. Evan's happiness? His peace?

"You don't seem like a quitter, Chloe."

She struggled for an answer. "It's difficult."

"If Thanksgiving wasn't this week, would you still feel like you need to go home?"

Chloe's mind had been filled with family, the fact that this would be the first Thanksgiving she'd left her mother on her own. "You get right to the heart of things, don't you?"

"It's hard to be away from family this time of year. But, this one time, don't you think it's worth it?"

Chloe stared down at her hands for a few moments, thinking about both Jimmy and Evan. "Can you tell me if there's something…bothering Evan? Something that's keeping him from accepting Jimmy?"

"He'll have to tell you that in his own time. But I can tell you that Evan needs Jimmy as much as the boy needs him."

So the bleak pain she'd seen on Evan's face was genuine. But did that make him more or less likely to change his mind?

Gordon shifted, reaching for his pipe, going through the quiet ritual of filling it with his favorite cherry tobacco, then tamping it down. "Do you believe in prayer, Chloe?"

"Yes," she answered without hesitation. "Before my mother got sick, church was a big part of my life. Since then…well, it's been difficult. But my faith's still strong, if that's what you're asking."

"Evan's isn't anymore. His faith has been shaken to the core. But, if he can reconnect to the Lord, I believe he'll look at Jimmy's guardianship in a whole different light."

Chloe felt the enormity of what Gordon was saying. Absently, she rubbed her forehead, remembering all the prayers she had uttered when her father was ill. When he died, she had been utterly bereft and confused. But Mom had made her understand that the Lord listened to our prayers and understood our hearts. That the illness hadn't been a punishment or a betrayal. Rather, they needed to cling even more tightly to their faith, to believe they would be reunited one day. Slowly, she raised her face. "What makes you think I can help?"

"Faith," Gordon replied simply.

It had buoyed Chloe at her lowest moments, when life had been so overwhelming she had been close to despair. She couldn't imagine living without it…or the pain Evan must feel without this most important anchor. Still… "I've been thinking about myself as well as Jimmy. About being away from my mother. But, even if I take that out of the equation…well, what if Evan never accepts Jimmy?" She gestured out the window to where Jimmy and Bailey continued playing. "You've seen Jimmy follow Evan around like a puppy. He'll be crushed."

"And if you take him back to the city?"

Chloe paused. Even though she had become too attached to Jimmy herself, her situation made it impossible for her to raise him. "I don't know."

"Do you think Evan would be good for Jimmy?"

Strangely, she didn't feel a moment's hesitation. Evan grumbled and continued to be formidable. But his dedication to his employees and family told her he was a good man. Chloe glanced again out the window. Bailey was utterly devoted to him. In her experience, children and pets seemed able to sense a person's character. "I don't think that's the issue," she answered honestly. "He has to *want* Jimmy."

"Which will take time. Repairing his faith won't happen in a few days."

Gordon was right. Fleetingly, she thought of her mother, how she had insisted that Chloe needed a life of her own. That was why her mom had urged her to help Jimmy. She was afraid Chloe was sacrificing her youth, her happiness. Her mom had also prayed about the issue and felt certain Chloe was meant to do this. She would be disappointed if Chloe returned prematurely. In fact, she had repeated that in their last phone conversation the day before.

"Chloe, I know what I'm asking isn't easy. You're miles from home at the most special time of the year. And, Evan isn't making our task any more pleasant."

She smiled faintly.

"Only the Lord knows our hearts."

"That's what my mother always says."

"Smart woman," Gordon declared. "Will you think it over?"

She could say no. Justify it even. But Chloe felt the Lord's urging. "Yes."

"Then we can get ready for Thanksgiving," Gordon declared.

Confused, she looked at him in question.

"Oh, we would have had the dinner. But now we have more reasons for giving thanks than I can count."

Evan helped Ned carry in the extra chairs. They had already extended the banquet-sized table as far as it would go. They would have their usual number of guests this year. Several people from the retirement home, plenty of others who were simply on their own. Employees, longtime friends, the table always overflowed with guests. This year, as many before it, they put up a second table to accommodate everyone.

The first Thanksgiving after his wife and son died, Evan hadn't wanted the dinner tradition to continue. But Gordon had prevailed on him to think of the people who were on their own who didn't have his choices.

Irrationally, Evan wished he could keep Robin's and Sean's chairs empty, knowing no one else should fill them. But his father's gentle guidance helped him accept the inevitable. Two retired employees, both widowers, now occupied those seats. It would have been difficult to see anyone in places once occupied by Robin and Sean, but these old, and now alone, friends helped ease the transition. Since his life now revolved around business rather than family, Evan was able to welcome everyone to Thanksgiving that year and the next.

Evan frowned. *Almost everyone.* Chloe and Jimmy didn't belong among old and trusted friends. He still had to learn the woman's true motive for sticking like a thorn. Jimmy...   The boy needed family, but Evan wasn't that family.

How many more years could he offer a full Thanksgiving table to his employees? If the business failed, he would no longer have the resources. And all of his people would be without jobs, possibly losing their homes. The weight settled in to a knot in his shoulders. He had to keep them solvent, keep them from losing everything.

Thelma pushed open the door to the kitchen. "You two hustle! I still have to set the table."

Evan had grown up with Thelma bossing him and didn't mind her orders. "Sure you don't want us to set it for you?"

Thelma plopped work-worn hands on her hips. "That's the first helpful thing you've said today."

Ned rolled his eyes, then followed his wife into the kitchen.

Evan angled the last chair into position.

"Wow. I didn't know there would be so many people," Chloe murmured from behind him.

He should have made his escape with Ned. "It's a tradition."

"Nice one. My family's small so we didn't have big celebrations."

"No extended family?"

"Not close by. My parents moved to Milwaukee before I was born. Their families stayed in rural Wisconsin."

"For a job?"

She nodded. "My dad's parents owned an apple orchard, but Dad was an engineer. So he had to go where the jobs were."

"Wisconsin makes me think of cheese, not fruit."

"We have a little of that, too," she replied drily. He silently acknowledged her subtle rebuke. "So what's rural Wisconsin like?"

"A lot like here, actually. Gentle, rolling hills, fruit orchards. More lakes than you can count." Reminiscing, she walked closer. "I spent my summers in the country with my grandparents. The city's great, but the country's…special."

When Chloe spoke, her eyes brightened, taking on the hue of green sapphires. It was the clear, clean green of fresh apples. Ironic, he mused, since she'd just spoken of the orchards. He remembered that her eyes could also ripen from jade to emerald. His gaze drifted to her mouth. Caught in her memories, Chloe's lips were almost like a kewpie doll's. The same lips that widened easily into a big smile. Catching himself, Evan stopped ruminating.

"Can I help?"

He frowned. "What?"

"With the table. I heard Thelma when I was coming in."

"Shouldn't you be watching Jimmy?"

"Your father is."

Evan searched for another excuse. Next to him, Bailey thumped his tail helpfully. "The plates are in the sideboard."

"Now I know why Thelma's been bustling around all week," Chloe mused. "All the baking, chopping…" Her voice turned nostalgic. "A real family gathering."

"Yeah. Well." Uncomfortable, Evan opened the silver chest, digging through pieces that had been in the Mitchell family for generations. Thelma wouldn't appreciate his actions. She had just polished all the flatware. Retrieving forks, spoons and butter knives, he piled them on the table.

Thelma pushed open the swinging door from the kitchen, assessing his actions. "You have to put the tablecloth on first."

Chloe smiled, then turned back to the sideboard.

Not that he cared about her opinion. Yet Evan snuck a quick look to see if she was still amused. She had one of those faces that looked perpetually happy. Oh, he'd seen a few angry expressions, but on the whole…

Chloe placed a stack of plates on the sideboard and turned to him. "Where do we find the tablecloth?"

"It's probably in the side kitchen."

She looked at him blankly.

"It's what city people call a butler's pantry where all the kitchen stuff is stored. It's next to the washroom. Thelma always washes and irons the tablecloth so it'll be fresh for the dinner, then lays it out in the side kitchen."

"Oh. I'll get it then." Chloe disappeared into the kitchen.

A few minutes later she reemerged, her petite figure nearly hidden by the huge tablecloth.

"You could have asked for help," he told her, lifting the linen cloth out of her arms. For a moment, he was face to face with her. Close enough to see the light sprinkle of freckles over her nose, the creamy smoothness of her skin.

Her gem-like eyes darkened to a near emerald shade. And he noticed the thready pulse at the base of her throat. Nerves? Or something else?

Long, dark lashes framed her eyes. Details he hadn't noticed? Or had ignored?

Abruptly, Evan stepped back. He had no need for these thoughts. Nor did he want them. His attraction to women had died with Robin. She had been the only woman for him and he had vowed to love her forever.

Echoing his movement, Chloe retreated as well, turning to the sideboard. "I don't know how many more plates to take down."

He cleared his throat, but his voice still sounded rusty. "Thelma has the exact count."

"I'll ask her then." In a rush, Chloe practically ran from the room.

Evan exhaled. His face felt warm, flushed. And he didn't intend to let it happen again.

By two o'clock the house was full of people. Chloe hadn't known exactly what to expect, but she was surprised by the variety of guests. Several elderly people, eager for the company, chatted nonstop.

Thelma's appetizers were a huge hit. Crab puffs, stuffed mushrooms, bacon-speared water chestnuts, red pepper cheese straws, tiny German onion tarts, spinach squares, mini pastries stuffed with locally made sausage. The enticing trays contained more food than Chloe could remember at any of her family holidays.

She recognized the man she had met at the Mitchell Company offices. "Mr. Perkin?"

"Miss Reed?"

"Chloe." She extended her hand. "It's nice to see a familiar face."

"Crowd gets a little bigger every year."

"Do many people from the company come for Thanksgiving?"

"The Mitchells collect strays. People who are alone, or don't have the means to buy a decent holiday dinner. And then just old friends."

"It's nice."

"Gordon started the tradition. Evan expanded it."

She was surprised. "Evan?"

Perkin nodded. "Where's the little boy?"

"With the older Mr. Mitchell. He's really taken a shine to Jimmy."

The man seemed to be appraising her. Chloe felt like she had on job interviews and had to fight the immediate desire to try and look more professional.

"Gordon's always been good with children."

Sensing no judgment in his words, she relaxed a fraction. "Jimmy's a great kid. He's fitting right in at the school."

Mr. Perkin popped a hot crab puff in his mouth. "Leaves you with a lot of time on your hands, I suppose."

"Yes, actually it does. I'm so used to being in an office ten hours a day—"

"Office?"

"Yes." She studied him, wondering at his interest. "I've had plenty of experience. I started while I was in college. Took all my classes in the evening." Chloe hesitated. "I'm sensing you asked for a reason."

"Not really. Just that we're shorthanded at the moment. One of our regulars is out on maternity leave. And, frankly, we can't afford a temporary replacement. We need to hold the job open for

Melanie because her husband lost his job. He stays home with the kids, at least until he finds something else."

"I'd be happy to help." The words flew from her mouth before she gave them thorough consideration. "I do have a lot of time on my hands. I would need to leave every day in time to pick up Jimmy from school, but in between..."

Mr. Perkin studied her again. "I might just take you up on that offer."

"I hope you will." As she spoke, Chloe realized it was true. Accustomed to being busy, she was restless between the time she dropped Jimmy off at school and then picked him up. Without anything concrete to fill the time, she found herself worrying about him. What if the other kids didn't treat him kindly? What if he got scared? Each day when Chloe picked Jimmy up, he felt more and more comfortable.

But the idle time allowed her thoughts to drift. And often in directions she didn't want—Evan intruded constantly on her thoughts. Chloe rationalized that it was because he was the one she had to convince, the one standing between Jimmy and his happiness. But, today, as she had stared into Evan's eyes, she'd wondered.

Drawn by her own thoughts, Chloe raised her face, trying to casually gaze around the room. But when her gaze stopped on Evan, she felt a peculiar pit in her stomach. Her breath shortened. Not wanting him to see her reaction, she turned suddenly. Fortunately, she turned in Jimmy's direction. Even though he stood next to Gordon, he looked overwhelmed by the crowd of strangers. Especially since Gordon spoke in turn with his guests.

Needing to reassure Jimmy, Chloe wove between the crush of people until she reached him. He immediately grabbed for her hand.

"Hey, big guy. I hardly know anyone here and I'm feeling a little lost. Mind if I hang out with you?"

He pressed closer. "It's okay."

Thelma raised her voice, and the crowd hushed. "Turkey's on the table!"

As people segregated into different parts of the dining room, Chloe anxiously looked for where she and Jimmy had been assigned to sit. She wasn't above switching some place cards if they had been separated. However, she was relieved to see that Jimmy had been seated on Gordon's right and her spot was beside her charge.

Gordon and Evan stood behind the chairs at each end of the table as their guests seated themselves. Chloe was relieved when Perry Perkin sat beside her. She guessed that Thelma had ferreted out the few people Chloe had met. Smoothing a linen napkin in her lap, she then helped Jimmy with his.

Glancing up, her gaze rested on Evan as he walked around the table, then paused behind two elderly ladies, stopping to talk to them and making both smile, then giggle.

Perry followed her gaze. "That's Gertrude Heine and Matilda Depson. Both are widowed."

"Did their husbands work for the Mitchells?"

"No. Evan knows them from church. Gertrude and Matilda are great friends, but as they've gotten older, their circumstances declined. Neither drives and they lived more than two miles apart. Physically, they couldn't walk that distance any longer. And living on only Social Security, they didn't have much money. Evan suggested they move to Orchard House, the Rosewood retirement home. But neither of the ladies could afford it. So, Evan insisted on paying their monthly fees."

Chloe knew how much that could be, what a relief it must be for the elderly widows. It was an incredibly generous gesture on Evan's part.

"Matilda and Gertrude worried constantly about their houses. And, neither one could physically or financially cope with keeping them up. Evan handled turning both places into rentals. He arranged for Gertrude and Matilda to have their favorite pieces of furniture moved to their rooms in Orchard House. Once they got settled there, Matilda and Gertrude had the best of both worlds. Enough that was familiar so they wouldn't feel they had left their entire lives behind. But now they don't have to maintain yards, and aging houses with a million problems."

Chloe admitted it was a brilliant plan. "And I suppose the rent helps pay for their fees at the retirement home."

"You'd think so, but Evan insisted they keep the rent money for themselves. He said he knew that ladies enjoyed buying a bauble or two every now and then."

Having trouble processing Evan's generosity, Chloe frowned. "What about their children? Don't they help?"

Perry shook his head. "Gertrude's daughter moved to California to pursue her music. She struggles just to support herself. Both of Matilda's sons are in the military. They do what they can, but being stationed thousands of miles away, it isn't enough."

"My brother's in the military so I understand." The pay was low, the responsibilities enormous.

"Matilda and Gertrude are happier than either one's been in years. The home organizes outings to all sorts of places. Twice a year they go to San Antonio, visit the Riverwalk or the missions. There's always something to do there. They went to a Spurs game last time."

Chloe grinned, imagining the widows in the midst of their enthusiasm at an NBA basketball game. They probably waved foam fingers and wore team ball caps and T-shirts.

"There are plenty of Mitchell employees here, though." Perry glanced toward the end of the table.

"The two older men sitting next to Evan are brothers who worked for the company until they retired. Then they fell for a scam targeting the elderly. Lost all their pension money. Evan helped them connect with the state's attorney. But they only recovered a fraction of what they lost. So, Evan insisted we keep making full pension payments to them. It's the right thing to do, he said. I admire Evan's honor and ethics, but as the financial officer, I have to admit his generosity is responsible for me going gray before my time."

Chloe glanced down, trying to absorb all that he had told her about Evan. Trying to compare it with the shell he had built around himself. To all appearances, he was all business, all shut away.

Then she wondered about Mr. Perkin himself. "And you? Is your family here?"

"I'm divorced." Although his voice remained calm, his eyes revealed a flash of pain. "My wife moved out of state, took our two children. I see them when I can, but this is her year to have them for the holidays."

"I'm sorry."

He sighed. "Me, too."

Impulsively, she touched his hand. "We don't always have to be in the same room, even the same state, to know our family loves us." Thinking of her mother, Chloe's throat clogged.

His voice was rugged, too. "I know."

Within a few minutes, Gordon and Evan both sat down and the group quieted.

Gordon bent his head to offer the blessing. "Dear Lord, thank you for each of these your children, our dear friends and family, gathered here today. Thank you for bringing us together, allowing us to be part of each other's lives. We are grateful for all the bounty you provide, the love you give us, the hope you keep constant. We ask that you let us remember and appreciate the true thanksgiving of each and every day, the blessings that surround us. Please bless and keep each of these dear friends safe and whole. We say these things in the name of your Son. Amen."

Amens chorused down the length of the big dining room table and carried over to the second.

Voices blended as platters were lifted, bowls were passed. Chloe couldn't stop thinking about Perry's words. And Evan's. About how the company was having financial worries. She took a scoop of mashed potatoes for herself and one for Jimmy. "Mr. Perkin—"

"Perry." He speared a piece of ham, then held the heavy dish for her.

"What would you think of Monday?" She picked up the meat fork. "For me to start helping out at the office?"

"I'd think that was the best offer I've had in some time."

Next, Chloe accepted a bowl of stuffing, offering it

first to Jimmy, then taking some for herself. Unable to stop herself, she glanced down the length of the table at Evan. Her thoughts were in confusion as she wondered about him, the real Evan.

"Perry, is there something about Evan's past? Something that…" She paused, seeing a sudden defensiveness in the man's eyes.

"What you want to know about Evan will have to come from him," Perry replied, circling the wagons around Evan like Gordon had done.

Chloe swallowed, wondering if Evan would ever tell her. Wondering if she dared ask.

Despite Thelma's protests, everyone insisted on helping with the cleanup. Dishes were scraped and stacked next to the huge porcelain double sinks. They had filled the dishwasher, but it would take at least a dozen loads to accommodate all the dinnerware and serving bowls. It was more efficient to hand wash most of them. Besides, Thelma insisted the good china wasn't to even get near the dishwasher.

They all carried platters and bowls of food into the kitchen, lining the counters and filling the table. Since Thelma knew where everything should go, she was in charge of wrapping the leftovers. And there were plenty despite sending everyone home with an overflowing plate of goodies.

But then Thelma had been cooking for days. She had roasted two golden twenty-five pound turkeys and a huge ham, prepared three kinds of potatoes, gravy, two kinds of dressing, yams, green beans, creamed pearl onions, homemade cranberry chutney, fruit salad, then baked plump yeast rolls and enough pies to outfit a bakery. Not to mention the slew of appetizers.

They set up an assembly line to do the dishes. Evan insisted on washing, Chloe was assigned to rinse, then Ned dried and handed the stacks of plates to Gordon who shuttled them into the dining room. Thelma had instructed Gordon to place the dishes on the table and not to try putting things away where she couldn't find them. Meanwhile, Jimmy ran underfoot, fetching and carrying.

One side of the sink was filled with hot, sudsy bubbles, the other with rinse water. Evan wasted little time digging into the mountain of dinnerware. Chloe kept up, swiping plates and saucers swiftly through her side of the sink. A few soap bubbles collected in the rinse water and she reached for the plug to drain the sink and fill it with fresh water.

As she did, Evan plopped a plate in her side of the sink. Realizing at the same moment, that it would fall to the bottom of the sink he grabbed for it. Having seen it coming, Chloe reached out at the same time. Evan's fingers closed around hers as they touched the plate. Chloe froze.

So did Evan.

Time stopped as their fingers grazed, the water

swishing around, encasing their hands in a liquid pool of sensation.

"Be careful with my crystal serving dishes," Thelma warned from behind them as she wrapped potatoes in plastic cling film at the counter.

They didn't jump apart. Instead, Chloe felt as though she moved in slow motion as she tightened her grip on the plate, then looked at the sink, the last of the draining water, the plug, anything but Evan.

He turned, immediately busying himself with another handful of saucers.

Ned and Jimmy talked in the background.

Gordon thumped down in one of the straight-back, oak chairs. "Thelma, you use more dishes every year."

"And you invite more people every year," she retorted mildly.

The buzz continued, but all Chloe could absorb was Evan's touch and the way it softened her bones, weakening them clear to her toes.

The porch out back was lit by soft gas lights and warmed by the round, full-bellied woodstove. Evan quietly walked across the aged oak planks, his thoughts confused, his emotions splintered.

Night was near silent, everyone and everything sated and tucked away. The sound of footsteps on the yellowing grass led to the broad steps of the porch. Instinctively, Evan stepped back into the shadows.

Chloe climbed the first stair. Sighing, she lifted her face. Platinum beams of moonlight cascaded over her face, enhancing her beauty. But also revealing her tears.

Evan emerged from the darkness. "What's wrong?"

Surprised to find him there, she looked embarrassed, then hid her eyes. "I'm missing my mother. I know it sounds foolish."

"If it's foolish to miss family, then the world's mad." Evan took her elbow and led Chloe to the porch swing where generations of Mitchells had retreated for comfort. He sat beside her, easing the swing into a gentle motion.

Chloe sniffled, another tear slipping down her face.

Unable to stop himself, Evan eased his thumb over her cheeks, wiping away the tears. Her skin was incredibly soft, just as soft as it looked. Unable to stop, his fingers cupped her chin, then tipped it upward.

Despite the dim light, he saw the confusion in her gem-like green eyes. Emeralds, he thought vaguely. So dark they resembled the finest of emeralds. When he didn't draw away, she quaked slightly beneath his touch.

Which made him wish to continue. Caution fled and he dipped his mouth to hers. Tender, welcoming, she kissed him back and he breathed in her clean vanilla scent. Tangling his fingers in her long, silky hair, he lengthened the kiss.

His conscience slammed into gear and he abruptly pulled away. *What was he doing? He had vowed to remain faithful to Robin forever.*

Chloe stared back at him, her lips trembling, her chest rising in short gasps.

Digging his heels in, he sprang from the swing. Not looking back, he disappeared out into the darkness. The comfort he had thought to offer had become his own. And now, it rose up in challenge.

Tempted by a harvest moon, he had betrayed the woman he had vowed to love forever. And he could never let it happen again.

The annual holiday bazaar was held on the Saturday after Thanksgiving. Established to raise money for those in need during the Christmas season, the craft fair filled Rosewood's park. People used the occasion to buy Christmas gifts, knowing the money was going to a worthy cause.

Chloe and Jimmy strolled through the mazes of booths, display tables and games. Not surprisingly, Jimmy wanted to play the games first. A scaled-down basketball toss appealed to him the most. Concentrating fiercely, Jimmy sunk three out of eight hoops. As a result, he had his choice of the second level of prizes. Again, his small face scrunched in thought. Finally, he picked a mug with the picture of a fish on its side. It seemed like an unusual choice for a small boy, but Chloe didn't want to say so. Maybe it reminded him of their fishing trip.

Their next stop was at the hat booth. From ball caps to an eccentric jester's hat with its jingling bell-tipped, floppy purple and gold arms, the shelves were crammed with novelty gear. Chloe tried on a sparkly green top hat that would be perfect for St. Patrick's day. Modeling it for Jimmy, she tipped to one side and bowed. He giggled and asked the vendor if he could try on a giant cowboy hat. The man obliged with a wink to Chloe.

Jimmy stuck it on his head, but the hat dwarfed his head, completely covering his face. "Nah, don't fit," he mumbled through the felt sides.

Laughing, Chloe spotted a smaller version. "How 'bout this one, pardner?"

The second one fit perfectly.

"Do you like it, Jimmy?"

"It's cool!"

Chloe dug in her wallet, handing the vendor some money.

"Don't we have to win it?" Jimmy asked.

"Not at this booth," she explained, accepting her change.

They walked on, pausing to toss pennies into glass milk bottles. Next, when they watched a balloon being twisted to resemble a dog, she cringed at the grating squeak, but smiled at Jimmy's grin when the clown handed the dog to him.

Reaching the area with handcrafted gifts, Chloe gazed around in delight. Piles of afghans, crocheted booties, children's clothing, knitted blankets, embroidered tablecloths and hand towels filled several tables. Booths displayed handmade jewelry, carved wooden boxes, metal sculptures, paintings, custom-molded candles, cakes, pies, cookies, ribbon-tied bags of homemade chocolates and other candies.

And the aromas! Every spare inch of the perimeter was crammed with food vendors of all kinds. Good old American hotdogs, cotton candy, popcorn, pizza, corn dogs, frozen bananas dipped in chocolate, hamburgers, funnel cakes, candied apples, and even deep fried dill pickles.

There was a long line at the bratwurst booth. Homemade sausage and sauerkraut in a bun was tempting, but then Chloe spotted kolaches advertised across the aisle. Milwaukee had also been settled in large part by German and Czech immigrants. Some of the German, Romanian and Hungarian areas still retained their ethnic identities. The Czechs had introduced their flavorful sweet and savory filled pockets of dough, kolaches, that remained popular. The savory sausage or ham kolaches made a meal. Various fruits as well as a cheesecake-like cream cheese filled the sweet ones. Apparently, they were equally popular in the hill country.

Her stomach rumbled, alerted by her inner cravings radar and they wandered closer.

"Jimmy, we have to try one." She read the selection. "I don't know how I'm going to decide." Eventually, they settled on cherry for Jimmy and cream cheese for her.

Finding one of many benches dotting the park, they settled down to eat their treats.

"Good?" Chloe asked.

He nodded vigorously.

They savored the kolaches while Chloe indulged in people watching. Lifting her gaze from a pair of adorable preschool-aged twin girls, she spotted Grace Brady approaching.

"Look! It's the nice teacher lady!" Jimmy exclaimed.

And she was. Grace had been kind, helpful and nonjudgmental about Chloe's mission to place Jimmy with an unwilling Evan. Grace saw them and waved. Jimmy hopped up, Chloe only seconds behind.

"Hi, you two! Enjoying the bazaar?"

"Completely! We just devoured kolaches. Honestly, I can just read the menu and I'm starving. It was terrible trying to pick just one."

Grace groaned, holding one hand to her stomach. "Same problem. I just left the popcorn booth. There are about a jillion flavors. I started out with cheddar cheese, then wound up stuffing myself with the white chocolate kind."

Chloe laughed. "Looks like we're going to have to visit there, Jimmy."

"Oh, and don't miss the booth with the oil essences. They mix whichever one you like into a natural sea salt scrub. My hands are so soft." She held them up, revealing a long, jagged scar. "Even around the scar tissue," she added unselfconsciously.

Gordon had told her about Grace's past after they met her at school that first day, moving Chloe to tears. Grace had been involved in a horrific car accident, resulting in devastating injuries. She had sacrificed herself by driving into a concrete barrier when another driver drifted into her lane, coming at her head on. If she hadn't, he and his family would have been killed. But Grace had paid a terrible price. In addition to internal injuries, one side of her face had been destroyed and her hands shattered. That was how she had met her husband, plastic surgeon Noah Brady. Fortunately, the multiple surgeries she had endured were successful. Grace's face showed no sign of what she had been through. All that visibly remained was the scar on her hand. Gordon said she had chosen to leave it to remind herself of what it had taken to bring her back to the Lord. Chloe thought it took an incredible person to come to that conclusion instead of self-pity.

Grace bent down to Jimmy's level. "How are you liking school?"

"It's okay," he replied with a shy smile.

"You know, I'm kind of new there, too. I just started teaching again when my little girl, Susie, was old enough for kindergarten, and that was the beginning of this school year." She straightened up, speaking to Chloe. "The school administration's been so great about it, adjusting my schedule to fit with Susie's. And it's nice to be able to peek in her classroom every little bit. Although she's just like her father, ready to tackle anything."

Chloe appreciated her new friend's kindness. Grace had peeked into Jimmy's room as well to make sure he was adjusting all right. At church, she had assured Chloe that he was getting on as well as he claimed. It put a portion of her anxiety to rest.

"Did you see Evan's booth yet?" Grace asked Jimmy.

"He has a booth?" Chloe was amazed. And uneasy. They had avoided each other since Thanksgiving night. But she couldn't rid her thoughts of their kiss. Replaying the moment over and over, she shivered each time at just the thought.

"It's for Mitchell Stone, but Evan always mans it. Except, of course, when…" She stopped abruptly, snapping her lips closed. Her look was apologetic.

Another circled wagon. Chloe longed to ask what Grace had left unsaid, but she couldn't in front of Jimmy.

He tugged at her sleeve. "Can we see Evan's booth?"

"I suppose so." She forced her voice to brighten, deciding she would act as though the kiss had never happened. "I'm sure we'll find it easily enough."

"Great to see you." Grace bent to Jimmy's level again. "Have a good time today."

Chloe and Jimmy strolled down the paths between displays, booths and vendors. It didn't take long to find Evan. A chronological history of Mitchell Stone in pictures papered the wall behind him. Generations of Mitchells, from a man standing next to the quarry with a pick ax to the present-day corporation. A wide shelf held a collection of exotic-looking gems. And all sorts of rocks filled the tables. Raw, beautiful chunks of amethyst sat next to elegantly carved onyx bookends.

Evan accepted the money for a set of intricately carved jade figurines from a pleased-looking couple, then stuffed the bills in a cash box. Glancing up, he saw them. His expression wavered between surprise and caution.

"We came to see your booth," Chloe began.

"Cool! Rocks!" Jimmy declared, pressing close to the stone display.

"Nice hat," Evan replied. He had taken a break to grab a soda when he'd seen Chloe and Jimmy trying on hats. She was completely natural and unaffected as she modeled some crazy green number, grinning and making faces at the youngster. Without the serious agenda she usually wore like an ever-present overcoat, Chloe appeared younger, more fun. It was a side to Chloe that Evan had never seen.

Jimmy plunked down a mug with the picture of a magnificent trout on its side. "Look what I won you, Evan!"

Taken aback, Evan looked at the boy. Apparently equally surprised, Chloe stared at them both.

"That's awful nice, but don't you want it for yourself?"

"Nuh-uh. It's 'cause you helped me catch the fish."

The boy grinned, waiting for a response.

"Nicest mug I've ever seen," Evan declared, his voice husky. "And I'll think about you whenever I drink a fish, I mean some coffee."

Jimmy giggled.

Not knowing what else to say, Evan placed the mug on the top display shelf where it wouldn't get damaged.

Chloe apparently sensed the awkward gap. "Look at this pretty rock, Jimmy." She gestured toward a huge amethyst.

Back on familiar ground, Evan touched the raw edge which had been cut to reveal the beauty of the stone's interior. "That's a fine example of amethyst. See how deep the purple color is?"

Fascinated, Jimmy nodded.

Evan turned and picked up another heavy rock, lifting it as though it weighed no more than an egg.

Chloe watched the play of his muscles beneath his shirt. He might work in an office, but the fact couldn't be proved by his physique.

"This is the same kind of stone." He pointed to the pale lavender striping. "This color isn't as valuable as the deeper purple."

Brow furrowed, Chloe studied the rock alongside Jimmy. "I didn't know that."

"Amethyst is a fairly common gem—it's a form of quartz."

Unaccountably nervous, trying not to think of their time together during Thanksgiving evening on the porch, Chloe fiddled with some small stones he had scattered around the table. Her fingers closed around a green one.

"That's a moss agate," Evan told her.

"Because it's green?"

"Could be red or black and still be classified as moss. There are several types of agate." He picked up a rust-colored stone cut and polished into an egg shape. "This is banded agate. See the distinct layers?" He indicated the white stripes that went around the carved egg. Then he turned, pointing to the large bookends she had admired. "Onyx is a form of agate."

Chloe shifted the stone in her hand, wondering if she could identify it again.

"Are those ones for sale?" Jimmy asked hopefully, looking over the array of small specimens.

"Which one do you like?" Evan queried.

Jimmy carefully studied each rock, finally settling on a smooth, polished, oblong-shaped stone.

Evan picked it up. "Good choice. Obsidian."

"Because it's black?" Chloe asked.

"They're usually black, but they can be red, brown. Green is rare." Evan studied the stone. "But actually they can even be clear."

"Do they come from your quarry?" Jimmy asked, palming the smooth stone.

"Nope. The quarry you saw is limestone. We own granite quarries, too. When granite is mined, it comes out in big, heavy pieces that are cut in to slabs. Obsidian comes out of lava flows and can be massive. Most precious jewels aren't that big."

"From lava flows?" Chloe asked, intrigued.

"It forms when viscous lava from volcanoes cools rapidly. It's about seventy percent silica."

Impressed, Jimmy stared up at him. "How do you know that?"

"In college, I studied geology. That's an earth science."

"We have science in school!"

"I loved science, and my dad taught me all about the rock business."

"So, you're a geologist?" Chloe questioned, as drawn in as Jimmy.

"I graduated with a double major—geology and business administration."

Made perfect sense. Impressed, Chloe toyed with the stone she still gripped. "Why do you have a booth at this fair?"

"To raise money for the town. People are always looking for unique gifts." Evan shrugged. "We like to do our part."

So much about this man was pulling Chloe in. Dangerously so. She had seen sides of him she wouldn't have believed existed only a few short weeks earlier. But which one was he? The hard man who could brusquely say no to a child? Or the one who took an interest in anyone who needed help?

And, what was his secret? The one everyone guarded so ferociously. A chill raced through Chloe. Could his secret be enough to convince her Evan wasn't the man who should take Jimmy in?

Chapter Seven

On Monday morning, entering Mitchell Stone, Chloe felt as nervous as she had on the first day of her first job. Jimmy was safely at school, she reminded herself. And, at the moment, Chloe wished she could join him.

"Chloe!" Perry Perkin greeted her cheerfully. "So, you didn't get scared off the idea over the weekend, I see."

"I need to keep busy," she replied, verbalizing the self-talk she had been reciting all morning.

"What's the majority of your background?"

She hesitated briefly. "Legal."

His eyebrows lifted a fraction. "What we need isn't nearly as exciting. To begin with, there's a mountain of filing."

"That's what I started out doing years ago. I don't mind." Actually, it was a good way to discover what the company was about. Learning the in and outs of filing systems had helped her leapfrog from general clerk to receptionist and eventually executive secretary at the law firm. A lot of businesses didn't employ secretaries as much any more. But, fortunately, in the legal profession, they were still in demand.

Perkin led her down the wide hall to a good-sized room. "Company started out with a half a dozen file cabinets, then moved the records into one cramped room. Even though we're supposed to be going paperless in this country, it hasn't happened yet. In addition to this file room, there's one upstairs on the second floor as well." Perry turned down another hall. "Let's head over this way." First he pointed out his own office and reminded Chloe where Evan's was. Then Perry showed her the cozy employee break room which had a microwave, dishwasher, snack machines, tables and comfortable-looking chairs. A long, overstuffed couch lined one wall. Perry opened the refrigerator, which was stocked with soda and juice, all free to the employees. As was coffee and tea.

"This is generous," Chloe commented, noticing a box of donuts on the counter.

"Treat people like you want to be treated and they're happier employees."

"Too bad all companies don't feel that way."

Perkin smiled with a touch of bemused exasperation. "Not even the economy tanking a few years ago could make Evan cut down any employee benefits or perks. I admire his ethics, but as the financial officer it does keep me up nights."

So, Evan had been completely truthful when he had told her about the company's financial difficulties. Initially, she had thought it was a convenient excuse—but, once again, the fact was reaffirmed.

Perkin showed her around, introducing Chloe to the receptionist, account managers, clerks and the office manager, Viola, who was going to train her.

"You'll meet production employees as they happen by," Perry explained. "Even though they work at the quarry, most stop by once in a while. Did you meet anyone on your tour?"

"Not really," she admitted, trying to tactfully phrase her explanation. "It was a rather quick tour."

He grinned, then glanced down the hall. "Here comes Viola now. If you need anything, let me know. You know where my office is and my extension is two-fifty-nine. There's a phone on every desk. We appreciate this, Chloe."

"My pleasure."

Viola, a cheerful woman in her early forties, made it clear she was delighted with the help. "You are a real trouper agreeing to tackle this filing."

"I can practically file in my sleep." Chloe grinned. "Not that I will."

Viola spent more than an hour outlining the basics of the system, then providing sorters so Chloe could begin to organize the tall stacks of invoices and correspondence. Then she showed Chloe to a desk near the window in the file area. "There's plenty of room to stow your purse and anything else you want to in the bottom desk drawer. Melanie cleared out her things before she left. I know she'll appreciate this. She really needs the job."

"That's what I heard. Since I'm in the same position with my own job, I completely understand."

Viola studied her for a moment. "Good then. There's a hook behind the door for your coat. I know Perry showed you around, but if you can't find something, just holler, okay?"

"Absolutely." Accustomed to working on her own for the senior partner of a large firm, Chloe had no problem understanding the system. And, as she sorted correspondence, she read Mitchell Stone's recent history. It seemed that Evan was working on a large deal that might be important. She hoped so. Not just for his sake, but for his employees. Chloe hated to think of anyone losing their job. She knew Evan wasn't the only employer who worried about his people, but too many cut employees rather than profits.

Several hours passed as Chloe categorized papers, dividing invoices to be filed in the numbered sorter by date, and correspondence to fit in an alphabetical one. It was a fairly big job and would probably take several days. And, of course, more paperwork was constantly being generated. She glanced at her watch. Time to go pick up Jimmy.

Gathering her purse and sweater, Chloe stopped by Viola's office to let her know she was leaving. "Oh, and I left the sorters on the desk so I can pick up tomorrow where I left off."

Viola looked relieved. "I should have explained that the rest of us are sharing Melanie's job. So, there is more to do than just filing, hopefully something more interesting."

"No complaints. I've yet to have an office job with absolutely no filing. I still file private and privileged correspondence in my job."

Viola looked at her strangely. "As an estate representative?"

Chloe bit her lip, wishing she didn't have to conceal her real job. "Estate work involves legal work, so…" She shifted her purse. "Anyway, I'll see you tomorrow."

"Good. And thanks again."

It took all of her control not to rush from the building. She had no talent for guile. Growing up with strict guidelines about telling the truth, misrepresenting herself was straining her nerves. Mr. Wainwright had articulated her mission as part of her ever-evolving job. But she didn't want to deceive these people. All of them had been kind and open with her.

Well. Almost all of them.

No one wanted to tell her about Evan's secret, perhaps from his past. She shouldn't be thinking of his past. She needed to concentrate on Jimmy's future. But Chloe had a strong feeling that the two were inescapably entwined.

"We're going to put stars and sprinkles and stuff on cupcakes," Jimmy told Chloe. "Then we get to go to the house where the old people live."

Evan noticed that Chloe seemed distracted.

"Chloe," Jimmy repeated.

"Yes. Um…cupcakes?"

"Can we get special sprinkles to put on them?"

She tried to collect herself. "I'm sure we can."

"When?"

"When do you need them?"

"Tomorrow." Jimmy's eyes glowed with excitement. The boy was gradually losing that pinched, anxious look.

Chloe blinked. "Tomorrow?"

Evan chuckled.

Drawing her eyebrows together, she frowned at him.

Coughing to disguise his laughter, Evan realized that for Chloe, not having children of her own, being with Jimmy day and night was a baptism by fire.

Chloe glanced at her watch. "We'd better go now, then, before everything closes. I guess the grocery store would have them—"

"And the bakery if you're in a pinch. You know where both are, don't you?"

She looked blank.

Evan wanted to smirk but the hopeful expression on Jimmy's face stopped him. Wasn't the boy's fault Chloe had dragged him to Rosewood. "We can go in my truck."

Looking relieved, Chloe grabbed her purse. As they piled in the truck, she encouraged Jimmy to get in first. So she wouldn't have to sit next to him?

The grocery store wasn't very busy, but the aisle with baking supplies was pretty crowded. Apparently, a few other kids in the first grade hadn't told their parents about cupcake decorating until the last minute as well.

Robin used to make the holiday season stretch out as long as possible. She baked over a dozen different kinds of cookies, but the most special times had been the ones when Sean helped her decorate. They'd had an entire arsenal of decorating supplies from chocolate sprinkles to pearl nonpareils. Robin had amassed a large collection of cookie cutters for every holiday of the year, but the copper Christmas ones were the most special. Lofty stars, elegant angels, and all the members of the nativity. Her cookie crêche had always been a marvel. Just as she had been.

Despite the time that had passed, the loss pierced fresh and new. This was the time of year for Evan to count his blessings, to be grateful to God for all he'd been given. If he hadn't been standing in the middle of the grocery store, Evan would have asked the Lord yet again why He'd had to take them. Unexpectedly, Evan felt a tug on his cuff.

"What's your favorite?" Jimmy asked.

Evan tried to concentrate. "I like the dragees— the little silver balls. But the colored sugar's good, too."

"I used to eat the little red cinnamon dots when we decorated cookies," Chloe confessed. "By the time we got to the gingerbread men, my mother would pull out the extra bag she had set aside, well, actually hidden, because she knew I'd nibble on too many every time."

"The sprinkles fall off sometimes." Jimmy looked suddenly worried.

"We'll buy enough to have plenty of extra ones," Chloe assured him. "They still have lots of colors left in the sugars. My mother said they used to only have red and green."

"How come?"

"People keep finding out new ways to make our favorite things even better. Personally, I like the pink-colored sugar."

Evan withheld a chuckle.

Chloe looked over a woman's shoulder at the display. It was a good selection. Bottles of sprinkles, lots of kinds—stars, hearts, confetti, tiny nonpareils.

Then she had a thought. "Are we supposed to bring the frosting?"

Jimmy shrugged his thin shoulders.

She scratched her head. "I'd better get cream cheese, powdered sugar, butter, vanilla—"

"I imagine Thelma has most of that in the pantry," Evan interrupted.

"Even so, she may have plans for her ingredients. This *is* the baking season."

So it seemed. Women were studying most every product in the aisle. A few men acted baffled as they searched for items on their lists.

"Could you stay with Jimmy while I collect the frosting ingredients?"

Evan wanted to refuse. Intended to. Then Jimmy looked up at him expectantly.

"Sure."

While Chloe disappeared into the land of cream cheese, he and Jimmy debated the merits of the decorating options, ultimately choosing almost every single kind. All but the pink. Then Jimmy's hand strayed back toward the bottle of pink sugar crystals. "Maybe I should make a pink one for Chloe."

It was the kind of gesture Sean would have made. Evan resented the sudden lump in his throat.

"Is that okay?" Jimmy asked.

He could only nod. Even though his father had opened the family home to Chloe and Jimmy, Evan wondered how much longer he could bear it. The memories flooded more often, more completely each day. After the accident, Evan had immersed himself in memories, clinging to each and every one. But then he had begun to push them away, to escape the pain. The pushing allowed him to cope, to function. Yet he didn't want to forget a single detail about either of them. But he had found himself studying Robin's photo more often lately, realizing her face had begun blurring in his memory. How, he couldn't understand. Yet it had.

"My goodness!" Chloe announced. "I thought you were going to *choose* some decorations."

Evan felt the need to get away. From Chloe. From Jimmy. From everything they were making him feel. "We did," he replied shortly.

She looked surprised. Not waiting to hear if she had anything to add, he wheeled the basket toward the checkout stand.

Refusing the guardianship, once and for all, couldn't wait any longer. He was going to speak to his father. And make him understand.

The following morning Gordon slept in. When Evan had returned from the grocery store with Chloe and Jimmy the previous evening, Gordon had already gone to bed. It was almost as though his father had some sort of radar alert. At the same time, Evan couldn't dispel his worry. What if his father's health was wavering?

Still, they had to talk. But Evan couldn't wait around the house until his father was up and around. First, he had a phone conference with their newest and now biggest customer. TEX-INC had just given them the largest order they had received in more than three years. TEX-INC was building several commercial complexes around the country that would house retail stores and restaurants, with a top floor of high-end condos. The consolidated concept appealed to people looking to reduce the time and cost of commuting. TEX-INC had targeted several big cities, purchasing land adjacent to the business districts. Since TEX-INC was based out of Houston, they were close enough to inspect Mitchell's materials and also have face-to-face meetings when needed.

The profit from this one order could offset more than three years of doing business in the red. Just staying even was a success, because the smaller orders were trickling in more often now. Coupled with a few more large deals, Mitchell Stone would be back on solid footing. And, with this order, Evan hoped to get one of the large national banks onboard.

Evan clicked off the phone conference, raising two thumbs in victory. Now, Perry could make an appointment with the national bank they'd agreed on. Skirting his desk, Evan whistled as he made his way to Perry's office. Glancing in the file room, Evan thought he caught a flash of long, caramel-colored curls. He was going to have to make sure he and his father had that talk right away.

Chloe trudged through the front door of the Mitchell house, tired after a long walk. She had left Jimmy playing in the backyard with Bailey, watched over by Thelma. Hours of filing invoices and receivables that day had given Chloe a clearer picture of Mitchell Stone's financial state. It was even worse than she had imagined. No wonder Evan was tense. While she hadn't yet seen any ledgers, she could add quickly enough to tell the outgoing far outweighed the money coming in.

Shrugging out of her sweater, Chloe paused, surprised to hear raised voices upstairs. Although the situation with Jimmy had caused plenty of tension, this was the first time she had heard any arguing. Uncomfortable about being able to overhear, she knew she couldn't go up to her room to change for dinner.

Chloe ran chilled fingers through her windblown hair. Thelma wouldn't mind what Chloe wore. The older woman was too down-to-earth to care about trivialities. Quick, hard boot steps hit the wooden stairs, reverberating throughout the entry hall. Chloe wanted to turn and escape through the kitchen, but whoever was coming down the staircase would see her.

Heart sinking, she was fairly certain those strident steps belonged to Evan. Still uncomfortable, she glanced up, hoping to remain unseen.

Evan looked livid. Brow furrowed, lips thinned, his neck flushed, Evan exuded anger. Unconsciously, Chloe took a step backward.

"There you are!" Evan accused.

"I was taking a—" she started to explain.

"Stay right there." He hit the last step with a forceful thud. "I want to talk to you."

Chloe had a strong feeling he wasn't going to just talk. Not with all the anger spilling out of him.

"Did you talk to my father today?" Evan demanded.

She opened her mouth.

But he cut her off. "Don't bother denying it. He was all ready for me."

Chloe could easily guess what they had been arguing about.

"Which part of *this isn't going to work* don't you understand?" He stepped even closer. "I've heard all your reasoning, but I told you mine. That isn't going to change."

Perplexed, she wondered what had set him off just now. "Did something happen?"

"You barged in here. After I'd told Wainwright no."

Chloe looked around uneasily. "Do you know where Jimmy is?"

She hadn't thought it was possible, but Evan looked even angrier. "Am *I* supposed to be keeping up with him now?"

Chloe lowered her voice. "I don't want him to hear us."

He threw up his hands. "You still can't seem to remember this is my house."

"I just—"

"Look, I've been patient. Now it's time—"

A muffled cry caught Chloe's attention and she turned.

"What—"

"Shush."

Evan jerked his head back in disbelief.

But Chloe was following the sound she had heard. Reaching the dining room, she spotted something on the floor and knelt to retrieve it.

"What…" Evan repeated. But his protest trailed to an end when he saw what Chloe had found.

A fully decorated cupcake dropped so that it had landed on its side and smushed the frosting.

Grimly, Chloe picked it up, glaring at Evan angrily. She had asked him to stop.

Glancing around, Evan wondered when the boy had come in to the dining room. "You think Jimmy heard?"

"You think there was any way he could avoid it?" Anger warred with disappointment in her face.

Guilt swamped Evan. He had never intended to

hurt Jimmy. How had he allowed himself to get in this position? He pushed through the swinging door to the kitchen, but the room was empty. "Did you leave Jimmy by himself?"

Indignation mounted on Chloe's face like a wind-whipped flag. "Of course not! He was playing out back with Bailey. Thelma was watching him."

Evan yanked open the door leading out to the porch, crossed it rapidly and searched the yard, spotting Thelma deadheading the last of the autumn chrysanthemums. "Thelma, do you know where Jimmy is?"

She turned around. "He's right..." Her watchful gaze swept the yard. "He was here just a minute ago. He must have gone inside."

That was what Evan was afraid of. Immediately, he ran through a mental inventory of all the places he had used as a kid to hide. Not wasting time explaining to Chloe, he strode toward the old carriage house. There was still a loft intact above where they now parked their vehicles. Once it had held hay. Now he hoped it held a small, seven-year-old boy. He quickly climbed the built-in wooden ladder. These days, only a few trunks were stored in the loft. Evan's breath shortened. A few of them were large enough to hold a small boy. But was there enough air in them for that same small boy?

Yanking open the lids, he quickly discovered that Jimmy hadn't climbed inside any of them. Nor was the child anywhere else in the loft. Evan descended the ladder quickly.

"He's not down here in the garage," Chloe told him, her eyes filled with worry.

"He can't have gone far." Evan headed next to the storage shed. In addition to practical items like a lawn mower and gardening tools, the shed held an array of implements that dated back to his great-grandfather's time. Plenty of places for a young child to wriggle under. But Jimmy was nowhere to be found. "He couldn't be in the attic," Evan muttered. "We would have seen him going upstairs."

"I thought the house had three staircases."

"Right. Still…" Evan stepped out of the shed, listening to the sounds carried in the light breeze. Abruptly, he turned, striding in the opposite direction.

Chloe's shorter legs pumped to catch up to him.

Evan skirted the back porch, sprinting to the side of the house where the wraparound porch continued. The yard sloped near the end of the porch, creating a nook beneath the wide planks. Evan remembered plenty of times as a kid when it had been his sanctuary. Like the day when, while playing in the Little League championships, he struck out, and his team lost. The times when a beloved pet had passed away. When his grandfather died.

Chloe caught up with him, walking by his side as they neared the secluded retreat. The spot was the farthest away from everything without leaving the property. The sound of muffled crying nearly stopped Evan in his tracks. Waves of memories hit. Sean's tears, his own. The ones still unshed mixed with both.

His hesitation allowed Chloe to shoot past. Kneeling down, she crawled beneath the porch, her petite frame easily fitting inside. Jimmy hugged his knees to his chest. Lips wobbling, he swiped at the tears running from red-rimmed eyes.

Instantly, Chloe gathered him close. "Oh, sweetheart, what is it?"

He cried even harder and Chloe glanced back at Evan. Then, she dug in the pocket of her jacket, retrieving a handkerchief. She gently dabbed Jimmy's cheeks.

Jimmy allowed her to wipe his face, then buried it against her shoulders, sobs rattling his small frame.

Evan felt horrible, utterly guilty. Kneeling down, he couldn't begin to fit his tall body beneath the porch, but he could reach in with his long arms. He patted Jimmy's back awkwardly at first, then in a remembered comforting way as he had done with his son.

Eventually, Jimmy's sobs slowed down until he was dragging in deep gulps of air. When he was quiet enough, Chloe stroked back the damp hair on his forehead, speaking quietly. "Did you hear something you didn't understand?"

He nodded against her shoulder.

"Sometimes grownups don't agree about things. That's all it was."

"Evan doesn't want me here."

As his gut knotted, Evan caught Chloe's loaded glance.

"Oh, honey, that's not true. We were talking about some grownup stuff, nothing to do with you." This time when she looked at Evan, her gaze was a hybrid of pleading and glaring. "Right, Evan?"

He swallowed. There was only one answer. Only one his conscience would allow. "Right." Evan couldn't stop looking at the hurt in Jimmy's eyes. "I've been worried about the business. It's on my mind all the time. Guess it just got to me today."

"Especially since I was working in his office today," Chloe added helpfully.

Startled, Evan jerked his gaze toward her.

"You know, like Perry suggested," she explained rapidly, inclining her head to tell him to agree.

"Right." *She had been in the office today?*

"Remember? I go there after I take you to school," she reminded Jimmy.

He looked up at Evan, a tiny bit of hope struggling to bloom in his face.

"To do… " Evan struggled "…office stuff."

"When I picked you up from school, we talked

about it," Chloe continued explaining in a soothing tone. "I filed lots and lots of papers."

Whose brilliant idea was that? Still, Evan was incredibly relieved to see Jimmy's tears stop.

"You know what? I was just about to go upstairs to change for dinner. Do you want to go up, too? Maybe splash some cold water on your face?" Chloe studied him hopefully.

Jimmy looked at her, then at Evan.

"Why don't you go ahead," Evan suggested. "We guys can wash up downstairs, right, Jimmy?"

Anxiously, Chloe watched for Jimmy's reaction.

He looked cautiously at Evan and sniffled. "I guess."

Chloe didn't look completely convinced. "Okay, big guy. I'll be down in a flash."

Evan extended his hand to Jimmy. When the small fingers curled in his hand, Evan had to quash the protective feeling that exploded. He held out his other hand to Chloe, helping her stand. Though he allowed her to take the lead in returning to the house, she dawdled, as though afraid to leave him alone with the boy.

The boy. He had to keep thinking that way or Jimmy would slip past his defenses. Once Chloe disappeared upstairs, he led Jimmy to the washroom in back of the kitchen. It was a plain, utilitarian space with a deep sink, soap and white cotton towels. The shelves held supplies, along with Thelma's own home-concocted soap they used when nothing else would clean motor oil or grease from their hands. "No frilly girl stuff in here." Evan grabbed a fresh washcloth and turned on the tap, letting cool water flow. Then he pulled out the stool that had been stored in the room since before Evan was born. "Hop on up."

Jimmy did, sticking his hands under the cool water, then splashing some toward his face. Evan smiled, seeing that the youngster had missed most of the tears, in fact most of his face. Still holding the washcloth, Evan placed it under the faucet, then wrung out the excess water. "Okay, turn toward me."

Obeying, Jimmy waited. Evan carefully wiped his face, removing all traces of his tears. Only the redness remaining in his eyes indicated his distress. "Sorry about arguing before. Like Chloe said, grown-ups make mistakes, too. I've sure made my share." Evan smoothed Jimmy's hair which was sticking out in every direction. "So, how'd your cupcake project go today?"

Jimmy ducked his head. "I brought you one, but it's probably all messed up now."

Evan remembered the dropped, now crushed cupcake. "You think you might want to decorate another one? Or maybe some cookies? I'll bet we could talk Thelma into whipping up a batch."

"Would she be mad?"

Hating that this child had to worry about such things, Evan shook his head. "Nah. She bakes lots of cookies during Christmas. She makes a killer frosting to put on them, too. We could ask her, then head over to the grocery store and grab a few more bottles of sprinkles."

Jimmy sniffled, then looked down as though studying his sneakers.

And Evan could feel his insecurity. "We can see if Chloe would go with us."

Jimmy lifted his face. "Okay."

"Now, we'd better go sweet-talk Thelma."

Chapter Eight

Chloe could scarcely believe they had wound up back on the baking aisle in the grocery store. She was even more stunned to realize Evan was planning to participate in the decorating. While they had been picking up supplies, Thelma had indeed whipped up a pan of sugar cookies and a large bowl of buttercream frosting. This was in addition to finishing dinner and serving it. Now a pan of gingerbread men was in the oven.

The first batch of sugar cookies cooled while they ate dinner. And somehow, Thelma had cleaned up the mess and also managed to arrange all the bottles and little plastic cups of assorted sprinkles, colored sanding sugar, dots and silver balls. Chloe didn't remember buying the little silver balls, but she did remember Evan saying they were his favorite. No doubt Thelma had a bottle of them tucked away in the pantry.

Freshly made frosting was divided in several small bowls so it could be tinted various colors. Bailey sat beside Evan, wagging his tail, staring hopefully at the cookies.

Jimmy's eyes widened when he saw the preparations. "Wow!"

Thelma chuckled. "We've had many a good time decorating cookies in this house." She affectionately batted Evan's arm. "And this one ate them almost as fast as he decorated them."

Chloe couldn't picture Evan as a boy. She couldn't imagine all his hard edges covering what had once been soft spots. But this house exuded warmth. Gordon was a loving father and she had never heard anything negative about Evan's late mother. Something must have changed him....

She watched as Evan reached up with one long arm to pluck a basket from the tall shelves.

His face went peculiar for a moment, then he seemed to shake it away, putting the basket on the table so that Jimmy could peek inside. "Next time, Thelma will let you pick some cutters and make the cookies in special shapes, if you promise to help clean up the mess."

Jimmy plucked a star-shaped cookie cutter from the basket. "Mommy had one like this."

That same peculiar look crossed over Evan's face again.

"We made cookies lots," Jimmy continued.

Seeing the bleak tension on Evan's face, Chloe stepped forward. "Then you'll know all about cleaning up the mess when you get to use these special cutters. What do you say we start on the first cookie?"

Jimmy didn't have any trouble deciding he wanted four colors of sugar. After he smoothed them in place, he heaped on sprinkles and dots. "Can we make another?"

Chloe glanced over at Evan, seeing he still looked upset. "Of course. What do you want to start with?"

Jimmy reached for a bowl of frosting.

"What color do you want to make it?"

His small eyebrows pulled together as he thought. "Can it just be white?"

"Sure."

Jimmy picked up the small offset spatula and carefully spread white frosting over the entire surface. Then he reached for the silver balls and carefully placed them so that they sparkled in all the right spots to form a star. As soon as he finished, Jimmy hopped off his chair, going to Evan's side, then tugging on his sleeve. The motion seemed to bring Evan back from wherever he had mentally traveled.

Jimmy looked up at him. "This one's for you, 'cause you like Thelma's frosting and the little silver things."

Evan stared first at the cookie, then at Jimmy. And something in his face changed. The hardness that never completely left his eyes dimmed. Though Chloe couldn't really believe it, she thought she glimpsed vulnerability there, too. "Well…" His voice was husky, almost gravelly. "That's fine…." He knelt down and accepted the cookie. "Mighty fine."

Chloe tried not to gape. It was a huge reaction for a small cookie.

Gordon strolled into the kitchen. "I can smell gingerbread men all the way to the den."

Pulling her gaze from Evan, Chloe glanced at the timer. "They'll be ready soon. Right now, we're decorating sugar cookies. Would you like to join us?"

Gordon glanced at Evan, then Jimmy. "I think I'll wait until the gingerbread men are done—they're my favorites." He took a glass from an upper cabinet and filled it with water. Turning back around slowly, he spoke to Chloe. "You know, the company hayride's this Friday night. Everyone brings their whole families. I thought maybe you and Jimmy would like to come along."

Chloe dared a peek at Evan. But she sensed he hadn't quite returned to normal. "It sounds nice."

"We always have a good time. The Markhams have a huge wagon and a strong team of horses. Someone usually brings a guitar, which we sing along with. Off-key, of course."

She smiled.

"Afterward there's a bonfire. Kids always like the whole shebang."

"The kid inside me thinks it sounds fun, too." Chloe realized she was growing nearly as fond of Gordon as... Her thoughts screeched to a halt. That train of thought had to be derailed fast.

After Gordon ambled out of the kitchen, she sat at the table and eventually both Jimmy and Evan joined her. She had thought Evan would disappear once the decorating began again. But he sat quietly, helping Jimmy tint the frosting green, then outlining a tree shape on the cookie with toothpicks.

Entranced, Jimmy carefully smoothed on the frosting, staying within the design for the most part. Then he embellished his Christmas tree with jimmies and multicolored nonpareils. His last touch was a small clump of silver balls for the star at the top.

"That's lovely," Chloe told him quietly.

"I wanna make an angel next. A Christmas angel."

Evan blinked. And the pained expression returned to his face.

Instinctively, Chloe realized Evan couldn't continue. "I'd like to help you with that, Jimmy. I think stars and angels are the very best designs for the season."

Evan's head rose, his guarded eyes meeting hers. He didn't speak.

Nor did she.

But, Chloe sensed that somehow they had just communicated more in the past hour than since she and Jimmy had arrived in Rosewood.

Full moons had their advantages, Evan reasoned, as the hayride began. But so did partial ones, like the slice of moon that lit the dirt road. At the same time, there wasn't so much light that every nuance of a person's expression could be read. Normally, it wasn't a concern. But he had been overly emotional since Jimmy had presented him with that special star cookie. Even though the child felt emotionally battered, Jimmy had reached out to him again. And Evan had nearly come undone.

It wasn't as though he hadn't faced any emotional encounters since his young family perished. Life hadn't stopped for everyone else when it had for him. But none of the others had been orphaned with only him as a possible guardian.

Equally unsettling was Chloe's surprising sensitivity, her understanding. Just when Evan thought he might crumble, she had reached out, diverted the disaster. She should have taken advantage of his sudden weakness, striking when he was vulnerable if she wanted to press her case, to accomplish what Wainwright had sent her to do.

Why hadn't she? The thought rolled around in his mind like a ceaseless pinball, striking curves, hitting flat out, but never disappearing. The few days before the hayride he had actually hidden out at his own office, unwilling to run into Chloe. Not certain what he would say if he did. But she had remained low-key as well, mostly staying in the file room. He overheard her speaking with the office manager, but left before Chloe could see him.

Hardly cold-blooded professional behavior. She could be off her game, but he didn't think so. Chloe continued to nurture and encourage Jimmy, and to further her relationships with everyone else in the house.

The clip-clop of horses' hooves blended with the quiet voices and occasional bursts of laughter from the wagon's passengers. He glanced over at Chloe and Jimmy, who were wearing newly purchased jeans and casual cotton shirts. He had heard her consult with Viola about what the attire should be. In addition, Chloe had made sure Jimmy was warmly dressed, insisting on a jacket and hat. But she wore only a light sweater.

The nights got nippy this time of year. Not the fierce cold of the northern midwest, but still cool enough to chill the bones. Everyone else on the wagon had been raised in and around Rosewood and knew the peculiarities of their own weather and had dressed accordingly.

Jimmy pointed toward the sky. "I can see really big stars."

Chloe smiled. "They're all big and bright in

Texas." She leaned close. "*Everything's* supposed to be bigger in Texas."

"I'm bigger," he announced.

She laughed. "Probably nearly a foot taller."

Jimmy grinned, then looked over at a group of kids his own age on the other side of the wagon.

Chloe followed his gaze. "Do you want to sit over there?"

"Can I?"

"Just remember what I told you. Have fun, but don't hang over the sides or back of the wagon."

"Okay." He took off like a shot.

Her smile turned tender. Jimmy had gotten to her. Why couldn't she have been the one with the opportunity to raise this loveable child?

Evan watched Jimmy scramble away, then studied Chloe's dreamy expression. "Think he'll mind you?"

"He's a good kid." She stared up toward the sky.

Evan couldn't ignore the sweep of Chloe's long lashes, the curve of her cheek, the fullness of her lips. His gaze lingered overly long at the last spot. "I know."

"I was teasing Jimmy," she said in a muted tone, "but the stars truly do seem brighter."

"The sky looks different everywhere. Altitude, air quality, proximity to artificial light…."

"That's the scientist in you. But as a Texan?"

"Definitely bigger and brighter."

Chloe laughed quietly. "The sky reminds me of how it looks back home at the lakes. Very different from the city."

"Which do you like better?"

"That's like asking which is cuter—puppies or kittens."

Amused, he relaxed a fraction. "Guess it *is* the scientist in me. Never compared newborn animals with astronomy."

"Surely you've seen them in the clouds," she protested mildly.

"Not during the night."

"Ah, so technical," Chloe teased. "I've seen every living thing in the clouds."

"Even microbes?"

She groaned. "You do know how to take the magic out of the night skies."

No. The romance. That's what he was obliterating. And, the fact that he needed to, alarmed him. Yet he didn't pull away. If anything, he slid the tiniest bit closer. "Magic is in the beholder."

"I thought that was love."

The word dangled between them, hovering like a harbinger of danger, perhaps even more.

Chloe shifted first, ostensibly to check on Jimmy who was laughing with the other kids, paying no attention to two tense adults.

It was ridiculous, Evan reasoned. Just because he

was a man and she was a woman. He couldn't quite complete the thought.

The wagon hit a bump, jostling Chloe, pressing her against his side. She didn't straighten up immediately, instead holding her breath. Lurching the other direction, the wagon took her away almost as quickly. Evan immediately missed the contact.

She hugged her arms, shivering.

"You should have worn something warmer."

"I didn't pack a coat. I thought..."

That he would have already said yes to keeping Jimmy. That she wouldn't be in Rosewood long enough to need winter wear.

"Why didn't you buy one when you got the jeans?"

Chloe glanced down. "I'm fine." There wasn't extra money in her budget for a new winter coat. Not until she received the raise Mr. Wainwright had promised if she fulfilled her mission. She had received an email from the administrator at her mother's retirement home. The rate was going up again, starting the following month. If Chloe was very, very careful she could squeeze it out of her budget. Fortunately, her utilities would be less since she wasn't home. But what if Evan stuck to his guns? What if she failed?

And what if she never forgot the solid feeling of his muscled body beside hers?

Chloe knew he was strong. She had seen the

muscles flex beneath his shirt sleeves, and she could never have missed the endless length of his legs. Her breath was so short, she wondered if it would return to normal.

Even if Evan wasn't off limits because he was a client, she couldn't trust her judgment any longer. She had actually believed her fiancé, Derek, had loved her, that they shared the same dreams and values. How could she have missed what must have been colossal clues?

And then there was Mom. Chloe could never leave her. Chip wouldn't be back in the states for at least two years. Then he could be stationed on the other side of the country or world. No, she was the only constant in her mother's life, the one Mom depended on.

The evidence was conclusive, inescapable and it made her heart ache.

Surreptitiously, she peeked over at Evan. He, too, looked as though he had more than stars and hay-rides on his mind.

There was something so basic, so appealing about bumping along a country road in the dark, wrapped in the comforting warmth of good people. For the briefest moment, Chloe let herself imagine how it would be if these were her friends, her family. Evan and Jimmy...family? The tender part of her heart twinged.

And she couldn't stop herself from lifting her

face to meet Evan's eyes. Despite the dim light of the night sky, she watched his eyes darken, shifting to another place, another mood. She swallowed. The wagon lurched and Chloe allowed herself to slide with the motion, her arm pressing against his. Although reluctant to lose contact, she twisted until she faced him.

His eyes darted to her lips.

Throat dry, mouth drier, she could only continue gazing at him.

Tilting his head ever so much, he leaned close. So close she felt his breath whisper over her. The chill of the night fell away.

Evan's mouth met hers, searching, settling into her lips, soft and strong, intoxicating and powerful. Somewhere, drifting in her thoughts, was the notion that she should pull away, remind him that this could go nowhere. That she was a completely temporary fixture in his life. Perhaps remind herself…

Instead, she waited until he ended the kiss, until he leaned back so that she could see his face. The regret.

Shakily, she inhaled. Was she doomed to go from mistake to worse mistake?

Evan looked as though he wanted to say something. Even though she had been hoping since she met him that he would speak more, now she couldn't bear a word. Not one single word.

Chapter Nine

Evan retreated to the den, warming his hands on a mug of coffee. Guilt filled, overflowed, brewing like the fresh coffee he'd just made. No worry that it would keep him up. There wouldn't be any sleep for him this night. He couldn't believe he had kissed Chloe again. Having almost convinced himself that it was an unintentional slip and vowing never to repeat it, all reason had fled when she lifted her face.

Sinking into a deep leather chair, Evan placed his coffee on the side table, staring at the portraits lining the wall. His great-grandparents, grandparents, then finally his father and mother. Each had taken the vow till death do us part. And each had kept it.

He and Robin had planned to sit for their portrait on their tenth anniversary. No longer newlyweds, but still early in what they assumed would be a decades-long marriage.

And he couldn't even keep the vow a single decade.

What was he thinking? Kissing another woman? The shame was overwhelming. He had ignored the Lord's voice since that fateful day when Robin and Sean had been killed. Now all Evan could hear was His censure. Dropping his face into his hands, Evan hated the other truth prodding him. That he had enjoyed the kiss. That he might even be developing feelings for Chloe. He groaned aloud.

"That's a mighty heavy load, son." Gordon's voice reached out from across the room.

Evan wasn't terribly surprised. His father had always seemed to know when he was needed. Slowly, he lifted his face. In the quiet, he could hear the tamping of fresh tobacco in his father's pipe. Not that Dad ever smoked it. He had given that up thirty years earlier. But he still enjoyed the ritual, the smell of his favorite blend.

"When you were a kid, you'd fall asleep in here, reading books about rocks, dinosaurs, and the Hardy Boys. Remember?"

Evan nodded.

Even though only one dim lamp lit the room, Gordon recognized the silent gesture. "Life's not quite like one of those Hardy Boys' mysteries. Not so easily solved, sure not wrapped up all tidy."

Evan sighed. "I know, Dad."

Gordon stood, relocating to the chair adjacent to Evan's. "I never wanted you to suffer so. When you were two days old, I promised you I'd never let anything hurt you. At the time, I thought I had the power to keep that promise. Took a lot of maturing to realize I couldn't. Only the Lord can hold you in His hands. And He does."

Assaulted by guilt and indecision, Evan doubted it. But hurting his father wouldn't help. "That's what you raised me to believe."

"Belief's a funny thing. It's easy when things are good."

Evan's defenses stirred. "You think I'm a rainy-day believer?"

"No man should outlive his child. And nothing hurts more than your child's pain. You're my child, Evan. Your pain is mine. I've felt it every day since you lost Robin and Sean. It's not belief you need to seek. It's acceptance, the reinforcement that you will see them again."

Staring at the floor, Evan wondered, as he had done since the accident. "Why them?"

"I don't know, son. But when the cancer took your mother, it was my faith that made it bearable, made me realize I could go on. Without it…" Gordon glanced up at the portrait of himself and Evan's mother. "I loved her all my life and I couldn't imagine life without her. Didn't want to."

"I'm sorry, Dad."

"We both lost her." Gordon tamped the unlit pipe again. "But I sure can't lose you."

"Don't think I'm going anywhere."

"Without your faith, you'll die inside a little bit at a time. One day you'll wake up and nothing's left."

Evan picked up his cooling coffee. "I'm having a tough enough time just getting through today." The kiss he shared with Chloe pricked his conscience again.

"The hayride." It wasn't a question.

Evan blinked. "Did you intentionally push us together?"

"Good parents don't push. They lead."

And that wasn't even an answer.

"Got any more hot coffee?" Gordon asked.

"It'll keep you up."

Gordon smiled, his concern evident. "Thought you might like some company."

Acceptance. Was it a concept or a reality?

Rising, Evan carried his coffee into the kitchen, dumped out the cold dregs, filled his own and a second mug. He paused. Thelma hadn't closed the kitchen curtains. Staring into the darkness, he continued to wonder. What if? What if he hadn't booked the vacation? What if Robin and Sean had survived?

What if he hadn't met Chloe?

Hadn't kissed her?

Evan's hand strayed to his lips, remembering the softness, the scent of her. What if, Lord?

What if?

* * *

Chloe devoured the new stack of correspondence that had been plunked into the *To Be Filed* tray. Letters to and from TEX-INC, apparently a new customer. They painted a hopeful picture. The enormous order could put Mitchell Stone back in the black.

Bells jingled in the doorway. Viola popped through a few seconds later. "Time to decorate. Actually, past time."

Her mind filled with what she'd just read, Chloe frowned.

"For Christmas," Viola explained. "We usually put everything up right after Thanksgiving. Being short-handed and all, we waited." She shook the string of bells again. "We all fix up our own areas, then a few of us tackle the reception area. You game?"

Chloe had been thinking about the tiny tree she usually set up in her mother's room. The home would have one in the communal television room, but it wasn't the same. She put down the letter in her hand. "I'm game."

Viola led her to the break room where open boxes were scattered around the tables. Plastic holly trailed from one, wooden strings of cranberries from another. One box in the corner remained closed.

"That's the nativity set," Viola explained. "We set it up in reception. Gordon and Adele brought it back from the Holy Land. It's really special."

"Ours always was, too."

"Was?"

Chloe bit down on her lower lip. "We sold our family home a few years ago. My mother's in a care facility. And my brother and his family are stationed overseas. He's Army. So there's no place to set up the nativity. I kept it, though. That and the ornaments we made with our father." Ridiculously, she felt the sting of tears that she blinked back.

"It's an emotional time of year," Viola said quietly. "It's supposed to be. Would you help me set up the nativity this year?"

Chloe's lips trembled. "I'd love to."

"Good. And pick anything you want from the boxes to make the file room area festive. We all do, so stuff gets switched around each year. Everything except the nativity."

"Thank you, Viola."

The older woman paused, searched Chloe's face, then nodded. "See you in a bit."

Chloe chose a few simple pieces to arrange on her desk and the incoming records table. Her mind swirled with memories and anticipation. Memories of Christmases past, the kiss she had shared with Evan, the expression on his face….

And the anticipation of setting up a nativity for the first time in several years.

For Jimmy's sake, she also considered the reverberations of Mitchell Stone's new customer. If Evan felt his employees' futures were secure, maybe he would rethink his decision. Perhaps he would decide that his life would be fuller with Jimmy in it.

Then, of course, she could go home. No more missing her mother, no more endless images of Evan's regret, his distaste for her. No more Evan.

Chloe pushed back the hurt, reminding herself it was for the best. That, even if Evan had been attracted to her, they could have no future. She expected the rationalization to make things better, to make the hurt go away. Yet it lingered, and it grew.

The day dragged along. Chloe popped into Viola's office to ask when they would be setting up the nativity. Learning it was just after closing time, she left to pick up Jimmy from school and get him settled before returning.

The days were growing shorter, the sun setting earlier and earlier. Driving down Main Street, Chloe felt nostalgic as she saw the lights, which were strung across the road, flicker on. A huge star dominated the middle of Main Street. Alongside, on the sidewalk, living Christmas trees were placed about every twenty-five feet. How long had it been since she had taken time to enjoy the signs of the season? Always in a rush from her job to the apartment or retirement home, she never noticed anything but red lights and stop signs.

Pulling in one of the diagonal spaces in front of Mitchell Stone, Chloe parked. She could see Viola and the receptionist, Jackie, through the large plate-glass window.

Once inside, she shrugged out of her jacket. "Hope I'm not late."

"Just on time," Viola replied cheerfully. The box containing the nativity was perched solidly on the counter. "We keep this area simple, tasteful."

Jackie, who had been humming "Joy To the World," set up a brass easel. "This holds our greeting cards."

A simple wooden table, topped by marble from Mitchell Stone's own quarry, had been placed between the two leather couches. Chloe tried to remember where she had seen the piece of furniture before.

Viola opened a package of dried moss, then pointed to a small box. "The straw's in there. Do you want to set up the stable and arrange the straw? You'll have to take out the other figurines first."

Taking a deep breath, Chloe realized she was being given the privilege of opening the nativity box. Carefully she reached inside, removing the first of several pieces wrapped in tissue. One by one she unwrapped the glorious wood figures. She paused when she held the manger. The quality of the carving was exquisite, replicating the rustic resting place of the Christ child.

Chloe took out small handfuls of straw, placing the chaff inside the stable. She centered the manger, then placed Mary on one side, Joseph on the other. As she finished placing the holy family, the entire scene came to life.

Chloe added the shepherds, then the Magi. Oxen, sheep and camel completed the last semicircle around the stable. Now, to place the babe in the manger. A lump stuck in her throat.

"Looks beautiful," Viola said quietly. "Every year, when it's set up, I'm moved all over again."

"My mother would be pleased," Chloe murmured. "Thank you for letting me be part of this."

"It's gotten cliché, the saying that people who work together are like a family. But we really are, have been for four generations. My great-grandfather was one of the originals. And, someone in my family has worked here ever since."

"It's rare—this complete devotion to the welfare of the employees. I'm lucky. I have a good boss, too. But this… You're right. It is family." Brow furrowing, Chloe frowned.

"What is it?"

"Just that family is so important to the Mitchells, yet Evan's so resistant to Jimmy."

Viola studied her and Chloe wondered at the doubt in her eyes.

"You've put it in a nutshell," Viola finally replied. "Family is everything to Evan." She walked to the light switch and flipped on the exterior one. Soft white lights surrounding the main window flickered, then settled to a gentle glow.

And Chloe knew she wouldn't learn anything about Evan's past from Viola. It was frustrating, yet she had to admire the loyalty of his friends, family and employees. Perhaps there was one person who would tell her. One person who had once been new to the town herself.

Grace's free hour was at ten in the morning and she had readily agreed to meet Chloe at the café on Main Street for coffee and pie. Although Chloe loved coconut cream pie, she didn't pick up her fork.

Finishing a sip of coffee, Grace's eyes lingered on Chloe's untouched dessert. "It's wonderful getting out for a while and I love the pie, but I'm guessing that's not why you asked to meet."

Chloe hadn't dared tell Grace what she wanted over the phone. "You're the only person I've really talked to in Rosewood who isn't related to or works for Evan."

"Hmm…" Grace listened, holding the mug close to her lips, but not drinking.

"And I think you know what I want to ask. Everyone keeps alluding to some sort of secret about Evan…his past or some event. I don't know what it is, but I feel that it's what could be keeping him from accepting Jimmy." She leaned forward. "Yes, I'd like to know for myself, as well. I admit it. But

Jimmy's entire future is at stake, his happiness. I wouldn't ask if I…well, I could ask Evan. But he's not going to open that door for me."

Carefully, Grace set her cup in its saucer, staring down at the table. "It's not a secret. The whole town knows about it. But, it's such a source of pain…." Empathy filled Grace's blue-gray eyes. "I know something about pain, how long it takes for a person to heal."

Chloe waited while Grace struggled over repeating Evan's past.

"Evan was married."

An involuntary gasp escaped before Chloe could stop it.

"And he had a five-year-old son. Robin and Sean were his life. Evan and Robin were high school sweethearts, then both went to the University of Texas, too. They knew they were meant for each other from their first meeting. They were married a short time when they learned they were expecting a baby. I don't know of any child that has ever been more anticipated and loved since conception. Their family was the ideal I wanted for myself. I think a lot of other people felt the same way."

Trying to assimilate the revelation, Chloe remained silent.

"To surprise Robin for her birthday, Evan arranged a vacation for the family in Hawaii because Robin had always wanted to visit there. They had honeymooned at Catalina because it was closer and Evan had to get back to the university for his master's studies. Anyway, they flew to Hawaii and stayed on one of the smaller islands. On the second day of their trip, they went to the beach. It was a gorgeous, out of the way area. And there was only one place to rent umbrellas and that sort of thing. Evan walked down the road to rent life jackets, chairs and a float for Sean. While he was gone, Sean got away from Robin and ran out into the water."

Chloe paled, feeling herself shaking inside.

"Robin wasn't much of a swimmer but she went in after him. Because it wasn't a crowded spot there wasn't a lifeguard on duty. Warning signs were posted, but Evan hadn't expected Sean to dash into the water on his own. Evan was only gone a few minutes, but the waves were huge, ferocious. The people on the beach noticed and tried to help, but Robin and Sean were swept out too far."

Chloe held one hand over her mouth.

"Evan dove in after them, but it was too late. The people there said he fought like a madman to get to them, finally retrieving their bodies. But it was too late. They couldn't be resuscitated."

"How awful!" Chloe whispered, tears gathering in her eyes.

"Evan blamed himself. He had planned the vacation. He had left them alone while he went to the rental stand."

"But it wasn't his fault!"

"He can't get beyond that day."

"I think…" Chloe began haltingly. "…that's what I see in his eyes."

Grace nodded. "His heart is broken. And so is his faith."

Chloe stared, unseeing, into the black depths of her coffee cup.

"My experience is different, but I found myself in the same place with my faith. It's difficult to… reconnect." Absently, she rubbed the scar on her hand. "Evan's been surrounded by people who care for him ever since the accident." Grace sighed. "I had to find my path myself, to accept. I couldn't understand until then. I thought the Lord was punishing me, abandoning me. I honestly don't know if that's how Evan feels." She placed her scarred hand over Chloe's. "But his pain must be mixed with fear. How can he love again? Especially a vulnerable child?"

Chloe couldn't begin to imagine the depth of his pain. "Why didn't he just tell me?"

"Maybe there's a tiny part of him that *wants* to accept Jimmy. He's a good and caring man. I suspect it was easier to say no by phone or letter. Seeing the little guy in person must have torn him up."

"He didn't show it…." Chloe met Grace's concerned gaze. "It must have been awful trying to keep that inside, especially since I've done everything I could to push Jimmy in his direction."

"Evan's bent, but not completely broken. It's that strength he has to hold fast to."

Chloe was shattered. What about Jimmy? His future? At the same time, her heart ached for Evan. And he'd never shared one word of his pain. "I probably would have gone right back to Milwaukee if I'd known."

A certain wisdom gathered in Grace's eyes. "The Lord knew that."

Had Mr. Wainwright? He had told her that Evan was single, not widowed, with no mention of the son he had lost. Had her boss hoped that Evan would see past his pain to take in another child?

"I'll pray for all three of you," Grace promised. "The Lord doesn't want little Jimmy to be alone, either."

Drained by the enormous discovery, Chloe found herself tearing up again. "I would appreciate that. I have some praying of my own to do. What if I should never have come here? Maybe, knowing this, I should go back now."

"And Jimmy?"

That was the killer. And Chloe couldn't help wondering if Evan needed Jimmy as much as the child needed him.

Chapter Ten

Gordon refused to let anyone off the hook, insisting they all gather in the parlor to decorate the tall native pine tree. Ned had hauled down several boxes of ornaments, lights, tinsel, and beading from the attic.

The living Christmas tree had been grown by a local horticulturist, Bret Conway, who avidly practiced conservation. He and his wife, Samantha, operated a family nursery. And each year, they delivered the tree, then picked it up after the new year. Gordon had been one of Bret's first customers for his living trees and now theirs was a tall, full, beautiful specimen.

"Does it get bigger every year?" Jimmy asked.

"Sure does," Gordon replied. "And we don't have to cut down another tree every year. The planet needs all the trees it has and then some."

"That's what my daddy said."

Evan watched their exchange, pleased that Jimmy seemed more relaxed. But that very fact worried him equally. His gaze roamed over to Chloe, who had been studiously avoiding him since the night of the hayride. She seemed quieter than usual.

Following Gordon's suggestion, she was carefully unwrapping ornaments that had been in his family longer than Evan had. The oldest were hand-blown glass, some imported from Germany and Poland. Others had been made by various family members. Those varied from childish paper cutouts to elaborately decorated salt dough, even a few crocheted snowflakes.

When she reached the one he both anticipated and dreaded, Chloe paused. It was a paper star that Sean had pasted his last photo on. People had always said that Sean was Evan's spitting image. Perhaps that's what Chloe would believe—that it was a photo of Evan. She studied it an overly long time, then placed the paper ornament by itself on a nearby table.

Her cautious attention to that particular handmade ornament made him wonder. Had his father spilled his guts? Wouldn't surprise him. Telling Chloe all about Evan's unfortunate past. Staring at Chloe deliberately enough to cause her to notice him didn't work. She avoided his gaze. Was that because she now knew more? Or because she regretted the kiss?

Eating breakfast and leaving for the office before

the others came downstairs, then making certain he and she never met at work, along with skipping family dinner had kept them apart. If Chloe had wanted to confront him, Evan hadn't been available.

Jimmy watched as each ornament came into view. Some caused him to raise his eyebrows, widen his eyes, or light up.

Chloe selected a bell made from tin and handed it to Jimmy. "Why don't you ask Uncle Gordon where to hang this?"

"Anywhere he wants," Gordon replied. "We just put them up wherever they look good. And, we usually add a few new ones each year." He smiled, remembering. "Evan's mother did have a strict rule about stringing the lights, though. Have to start at the top of the tree. Made me restring them more times than I can count."

Evan knew his father was missing her. "And, she made *us* untangle them."

"They had to be the first thing on the tree," Gordon added.

Chloe lifted the lights from a second box. "Funny how they seem to tangle themselves just sitting in the box."

"Really?" Jimmy asked, peering inside.

She smiled gently. "No. We're usually in more of a hurry to get the lights back in the box than when we take them out. So, they're easier to tangle."

"Oh."

A magical fairy that tangled the lights was probably more exciting, Evan mused.

Chloe held up one string of lights, starting to straighten it out.

"Why don't you help her, son?" Gordon suggested. "Jimmy and I can get out the garlands."

Reluctantly, Evan rose. "Want me to take those?"

Chloe kept her gaze on the lights. "I could use some help."

Still reluctant, Evan sat on the opposite end of the couch. It might be his imagination, but the lights were more tangled than ever. To reach the cording, he had to slide over one cushion closer. Chloe fumbled with the string, unable to find a starting point. Reaching to find it, Evan's hand collided with hers. As quickly, she pulled back, as though stung.

This time she didn't meet his eyes, instead trying to avoid them. Oh, yeah. Something was up.

Thelma bustled into the room, carrying a large bowl. "Who's going to string popcorn?"

Chloe glanced up at her.

"You're elected," Thelma decreed. "It's not hard, just pull a needle and thread through a piece at a time."

"My mother taught me," Chloe replied, accepting the popcorn.

Jimmy ran over and peered down at the overflowing dish. "Can I have some?"

"Sure."

He popped a piece in his mouth, chewed, then frowned. "It tastes funny."

Thelma grinned. "That's cause it doesn't have any salt or butter. You don't salt popcorn you're going to string. Makes it crumble. And the butter... well you can just imagine how hard it would be to string it all greased up. There's another bowl in the kitchen, one I made for you to eat. Want to go get it?"

"Does it have the good stuff?"

She plopped her hands on her hips. "I said it was for eating."

Jimmy grinned and took off for the kitchen.

As he did, Chloe used the excuse of the new chore to leave the couch and settle in a chair, placing the bowl of popcorn on a side table. Threading the needle Thelma had provided, Chloe began stringing the cooled popcorn.

With the fire blazing in the tall limestone fireplace, it could have been a Norman Rockwell sketch. But they weren't united. Odds and ends, all of them. He and his father, widowers. Jimmy orphaned. Chloe... Yes, what about Chloe?

Evan finally got the lights untangled, then strung on the tree. Gordon and Jimmy joined him, ready to hang ornaments.

Thelma came back into the parlor. "I'll string the rest," she told Chloe, picking up the bowl. "You go help the others with the ornaments."

"But I can—"

"Go on."

Chloe didn't hurry, finally edging behind Gordon.

Spotting her, Gordon pulled Chloe forward. "Grab an ornament."

She hesitated, then withdrew a small crystal angel. Evan barely contained his surprise. His mother's favorite ornament. Chloe reached upward. His gaze followed. She affixed the hook, then slowly met his eyes. Hers were filled with something he had never seen before. Evan sensed she wanted to turn away, wanted to run.

Seeing how Chloe had woven herself and Jimmy into their lives, his blood chilled. People close to him didn't fare well. And, Jimmy was becoming too comfortable, too attached. It wasn't right. The child would be crushed with disappointment when Evan had to send him home. Despite Chloe's tenacity, that would still be the end result.

His heart twinged, but he had to ignore the temporal feeling. Jimmy would be better off in a two-parent home, one not fraught with tragedy and guilt. Watching Chloe, Evan knew it was time to tell her so.

The homey warmth of the evening resonated in Chloe's thoughts. A memory maker, her mother would have called it. Seeing Jimmy's happiness.

Appreciating all the family times that had been experienced in the Mitchells' house. Especially knowing the pain Evan carried.

How did he bear to perform the same traditions he had shared with his wife and son? Chloe couldn't get the picture of Sean out of her thoughts, his sweet face, his bright eyes. A child who should have had a long and wonderful future. No wonder Evan had resented her sudden appearance on his doorstep.

But could he overcome the past? Build a future with Jimmy?

After pouring a cup of Thelma's spiced cider, Chloe turned around. And met Evan's glower.

It was time, Evan reminded himself. Time to set things straight.

"What's wrong?" Chloe asked.

"You. And Jimmy."

She hesitated, fiddling with a mug. "Your father—"

"Regardless of what he says, this isn't going to work."

Chloe's face filled with distress.

"There's no time in my life to indulge Wainwright's whims. I'm trying to keep a business alive."

She opened her mouth, then closed it as quickly.

"Oh, I appreciate you pitching in at the office."

"I wanted to," she rushed to say.

"Even so, you need to find another option for Jimmy."

"It's a cruel time to—"

"You think I'm cruel? Every day Jimmy's here, you're giving him false hope."

Chloe looked stricken.

And that bothered him far more than it should. "I've had my say." Unable to watch her despair any longer, he turned on his heel and left the kitchen. Once back in the entry hall, Evan expelled a deep breath. The confrontation had affected him more than it should. He started toward the staircase, then stopped. Pain mixed with guilt, then multiplied. Why did Wainwright have to disregard his wishes in the first place?

Sighing, Evan turned back to the parlor. Everyone had cleared out earlier. Only the lights on the tree lit the room. But he could have navigated the parlor blindfolded.

He stopped next to the table with Sean's paper ornament.

"I made it for you, Daddy!"

"All by yourself?"

"Mommy helped."

"It's great, big guy."

Evan swallowed, then picked up the small piece of construction paper, tracing his fingers over Sean's photo. *I miss you, son. I always will.*

With the greatest care, he carried the precious

ornament over to the tree, gently hanging it high on the top branch, close to the angel topping the conifer, her wings stretched out to protect all beneath them. "Sleep well, little angel. Daddy loves you."

Pushing the back of his hand against his lips, he stopped their trembling. But nothing could deter the tears stinging his eyes.

Chloe straightened the quilt on Jimmy's bed, pulling it up to cover his shoulders, tucking it in snugly the way he liked. Elbert had fallen on the floor, no doubt when Jimmy had kicked the covers askew. Despite his progress, Jimmy was still a small boy in a home he knew wasn't his own.

Tucking Elbert next to Jimmy, she sighed. Part of her wished she hadn't learned Evan's terrible secret. Her empathy was overtaking her objectivity. It wasn't just Evan's future, she kept reminding herself. It was Jimmy's. But could a man who had lost so much have anything left to give?

Crossing over to the bay window, Chloe looked out into the street. A tree in the window of a neighboring house caught her eye. It was quiet, families all tucked in for the night, children sleeping, adults easing into the later hours.

Would she ever have a family of her own? A child to tuck in bed? A husband to love? Her gaze strayed toward Jimmy. He had attached himself to her heart—it was no longer just empathy.

The lights in the tree across the street winked in the muted darkness. Closing her eyes against the reminder, she acknowledged what else was building in her heart. More than empathy for Evan. Far more.

Chapter Eleven

Evan's cell phone rang. Seeing it was his father, he answered quickly. "Hey, Dad."

"Didn't see you at breakfast."

No. And that way Evan hadn't seen Chloe or Jimmy.

"I'll take your silence to mean yes. Church school called. They asked if we could supply them with a boulder to use in their school play."

Evan frowned. "Don't they usually make them out of papier-mâché?"

"Not when children are sitting on them. It's for the little shepherd boy when he sees the star."

"Right. How big a boulder do they need?"

"The shepherd boy is probably six or seven. Principal said it's usually a first grader."

"Okay, Dad. When do they need it?"

"I told them today."

Sighing, Evan counted to ten.

"Of course," Gordon continued. "I suppose I could try and lift it myself…."

Pure blackmail. "I'm not that far from the quarry." Evan checked his watch. "Will an hour or so work?"

"Sounds good. Rehearsals start after school today."

"Okay."

"Son?"

Evan waited.

"I'll try not to volunteer you for anything else." Gordon paused. "Today."

Clicking the phone off, Evan smiled for the first time since his talk with Chloe. It didn't take long to drive to the quarry and load a decent-sized boulder along with a flat dolly to transfer it inside the school auditorium.

Funny how schools all had that same smell—chalk and cafeteria food combined with stale gym socks. Having attended the school himself, Evan knew his way around. He pushed the dolly over wooden floors, the weight of the boulder causing them to creak. The noise was going to make it difficult to execute a quick drop and run without anyone noticing him. He glanced around. Class must be in session since the halls were empty. Maybe the getaway was possible.

Children's voices emerged from the open doors

of the auditorium. A teacher clapped her hands. "I need the lamb and camel."

Two youngsters bounced up to the stage. The teacher showed them where they would stand. Both stepped outside of the chalk circles she had drawn. "Children!"

Amused, Evan pushed the dolly to the stage. Lifting the heavy boulder, he carried it up the three short steps.

The teacher paused. "Evan! That must weigh a ton."

It *was* getting heavy. "If you'll tell me where it goes…"

Flustered, she looked around. "Well…the night of the play it needs to be in the center of the stage, but it would be in the way for the rest of the performance."

Evan carried the boulder to the far side of the small stage. "It can be moved to the center on the night of the play."

"You'd do that?" the teacher exclaimed. "That would be wonderful!"

He hadn't intended to offer, but submitted to the inevitable. "Fax the date and time over to Mitchell Stone." The boulder in place, he turned around. And stared at Chloe. Who was supposed to be out of Rosewood by now.

Chloe stared back.

"Evan!" Jimmy hollered, running onto the stage.

"No running," the teacher chided.

"Guess what? I'm gonna be the shepherd boy. I get to sit on the big rock!"

Evan looked into the youngster's eager face and couldn't disappoint him. "Congratulations. I hear that's a big part."

Relief flooded Chloe's face.

Had she completely forgotten what he'd told her? That it was time for her to return Jimmy to Milwaukee?

"Jimmy," the teacher called. "Let's try out that big rock."

While he did, Evan pushed the dolly off the stage, then headed straight for Chloe. He nodded his head toward the door. "I'll see you outside."

Tailgate down, he lifted the cumbersome dolly into the bed of the truck. Despite the noise, he heard Chloe's hesitant steps coming up behind him. Evan whirled around. "What did you do? Jimmy's already in too deep and now he's got a part in the school play?"

"*I* didn't give him the part."

"You also didn't tell him no."

She gaped at him. "Why don't you do that? Tell a thrilled little boy who just got one of best parts in the play that he can't be in it?"

"That's your job, not mine."

Chloe shook her head. "Oh, no. You want to crush his spirit, then you'll have to do the dirty work." Stomping off, she didn't look back.

Evan slammed the tailgate shut. How had he lost control of his own life? Angry, he forced himself not to speed as he drove to his only refuge—work. At least Chloe was occupied at the school and wouldn't be there.

His office fronted Main Street and he always left the blinds open so the natural light could enter. Standing by the window, Evan watched pedestrians walking the elm-lined street. Mothers with preschool-age children, two aging men clinging to their canes, an elderly couple arm in arm. It was easy to imagine Chloe as part of the tableau, walking along, her hand gripping Jimmy's.

Evan sighed. Sometimes it was difficult to live in a place with so much happiness. Especially now that he was on the outside looking in.

Someone knocked lightly on the door frame.

He didn't turn around. "Come in."

"Evan." Perry's voice was somber.

Pushing the kaleidoscope of images from his mind, he faced his friend and colleague. One look told him it was trouble.

Perry gripped the back of one armchair. "The financing."

Evan knew what was coming, but he couldn't believe it.

"Fell through."

There was nothing to say. A million things to say.

"Any other avenues?"

"I've been on the phone all day." Perry sighed, then pulled back the chair, sitting down. "I have a few more places to try."

"But you don't expect any better news."

Perry couldn't hide his discouragement.

"How much of the big order can we complete without it?"

"Evan—"

He waved away the words. Barely a dent. He'd known before he asked. "Contract penalty?"

Perry met his gaze. "It'll wipe out everything that's left."

Evan turned back to the window, seeing everyone going on as though nothing had just tipped the world. "How long can we make payroll before we notify TEX-INC?" He ran his hand up his forehead, then through his hair.

"It won't be long."

Christmas was closing in. If he could stretch the funds until it was past... "Work up the figures."

The other man's footsteps echoed over the granite floor as he left.

Refuge? Now this one was crumbling. Soon he would be a man with no safe harbor. And people he had known all his life were going to be without jobs.

How was he going to tell them? Evan remembered the solace of turning to the Lord for direction. His own personal war hadn't ended. But, could he keep up the battle when so much was at stake?

Chloe read Jimmy his favorite story twice, then three others before he nodded off. Now she tucked Elbert close. Jimmy didn't stir. He had fallen asleep hours earlier, but she couldn't stop checking on him.

What would happen if Evan remained steadfast about his decision? For all that she wanted to protect and nurture Jimmy, she didn't have the means. Even if she found the money for a babysitter, her time wasn't her own. Jimmy would end up being raised by the sitter.

The ache in her heart resonated. And what about Evan? Was he doomed to live alone, without love, without hope? She had pushed and fought against it, but he, too, had broached her defenses. Why? Of all the men in the world she could have fallen for? Why Evan Mitchell?

Taking a last, long look at the sleeping child, Chloe returned to her room. The fire was banked, her cup of Thelma's spiced cider long empty. But she was still restless. Thoughts continued spinning, encroaching. Gordon had been excited to hear about Jimmy's part in the Christmas play. Since Evan hadn't been there for dinner, she had been spared his displeasure.

The mantel clock struck midnight. It was pointless, unnecessary, but she wondered why Evan wasn't safely at home. Surely if there had been an accident at the quarry, Gordon would have been informed. In a town like Rosewood, the word would have spread quickly.

Chloe edged the curtain aside so she could look out into the street. There was something comforting about the tidiness of the quiet neighborhood. As she ruminated, Evan's truck came into sight. It was the old truck she and Jimmy had ridden in with him. The beater rumbled to a stop near the end of the driveway. Strange that he didn't park it in the garage. Continuing to watch, she saw him climb slowly out of the driver's side, then just as slowly approach the bench that curved around the ancient oak out front.

Straining to see, she wondered at his behavior. Evan always walked briskly, energetically. Now he slumped down on the bench. Worry hit like a well-placed arrow. Something was wrong.

Disregarding the hour, Chloe grabbed her sweater, glad she hadn't changed from her warm slacks yet. Skipping lightly down the stairs, she reached the front door. Caution prodded. What was she doing?

Refusing to listen to the inner warning, she stepped outside, quietly crossing the winter-dried lawn. A few feet away from Evan, she slowed, but didn't stop. "Evan?"

He raised his bleak face.

Immediately, her heart thudded in fear. "What is it?"

Evan only looked at her.

The fear intensified as she sat beside him. "Evan?"

"You know just when to hit, don't you?"

"I'm not here because I want something," Chloe implored. "I was worried when it got so late. Then... I saw you from the window. I can tell something's wrong."

He searched her face, his guard dropping. "Wrong is an understatement."

"The business."

"Good guess."

"No guess. You worry about your employees as though..." She almost said *children*. "As though they mean the world to you. It has to be something concerning them."

The soft gas lights illuminated his expression. "The big order we got from TEX-INC—we can't fill it."

"Maybe they'll negotiate a later delivery date. They took time choosing their supplier. Surely—"

"It's not the delivery. Our financing fell through."

Shocked, Chloe tried to fathom the implications. "Surely your bank has done business with Mitchell Stone for decades."

"Make that closer to a century. The local bank

didn't have the funds in this economic climate. We found a big national bank, thought it was a done deal."

"There are more banks!"

"With the same criteria. We've lost money for the last four years, not a banker's dream."

"You can't just give up." She searched her mind for alternatives.

Evan laughed bitterly. "Easy to say."

The difficulty of her own life for the last decade surfaced. "Hardly. Yours isn't the first business to falter. And you're not the only person to face difficulties. But you have to believe you can turn things around!"

"Believe? You *are* new here."

"What? So you're going to cave, let all your employees fend for themselves. I'm sure each of them will find a great paying job, be able to keep their homes, feed their children—"

"Stop! I've been fighting this battle for years. You waltz in here and—"

"*Waltz?* Did you actually say *waltz?* I came here scared to death for myself, for Jimmy, for everything that means anything to me. And now, I'm getting to know the people who work for you, liking them, wondering how they'll cope." Her chest heaved with fury and frustration. "And what about Gordon? He'll be devastated. He cares as much about these people as you do! And—"

Evan held up one hand. "I can't take another *and*."

Her anger deflated. Drained, she sat silent. No bird sang in the night to fill the quiet, no cars passed, no dogs barked.

"I suppose one of us should jump on a white horse, put on some armor," Evan said finally.

Chloe leaned back against the bark of the sturdy oak. "I'm not that good with horses."

He turned, scrutinizing her. "An hour ago I wouldn't have given ten cents toward taking another shot."

"Does that mean you're not giving up?"

"How did you do that? Turn everything around?"

She looked down, fiddling with her hands.

Evan stopped the motion, curling her hand in his larger one. Chloe swallowed, all too conscious of the nearby light that revealed her features, possibly even her feelings. He leaned closer. She'd thought her heart thudded before. Now it nearly jumped from her chest.

His lips touched, then covered hers. Sensation raced through her as though day might never dawn again, that she must take her fill this very instant.

Evan cupped the back of her head, twining his fingers in her long, loose hair. Somewhere not far away, a cat meowed loudly. But it was too late. Nothing could distract her now.

Chapter Twelve

Chloe studied the latest pile of correspondence regarding TEX-INC, taking notes on each key point. The growing stack of refusals from the banks was disheartening. But she had an idea. One of their law firm's clients was a large, privately owned bank, where Mr. Wainwright also sat on the board of directors. She prayed they could extend a loan that would save Mitchell Stone and its employees' jobs.

As a bonus, if Mr. Wainwright helped Mitchell Stone, Evan might reconsider his position on Jimmy. She didn't think of it as buying their way past his defenses. But if Evan didn't have the constant worry about the fate of his employees, he might be more open to an emotional commitment.

Swallowing, Chloe knew she was avoiding her own emotions. Evan's kiss lingered in her thoughts, nagged at her conscience. What was she doing kissing a man she couldn't possibly have a future with?

Logging the last of her comments in her laptop, Chloe didn't notice Viola until she was standing beside her desk. "Oh, hi."

Viola glanced at the computer.

"I'm just used to taking my notes this way. Beats shorthand any day."

"Shorthand?"

Chloe realized her slip. "Typing fast is probably my strongest office skill."

"I don't know. You caught on to our file system in no time."

"Like I said, I know my way around the office."

"Right. In a law firm. Perry mentioned that's your background."

Chloe couldn't lie to this woman. So she nodded.

"Legal secretaries make pretty good money. Guess estate reps must do even better." Viola smiled, deposited a small stack of papers on top of the incoming tray and left.

That was close. She didn't need to complicate things now. Chloe scribbled a note on her desk calendar so she'd remember to check back with Mr. Wainwright the next day.

She glanced at her watch—an hour until she picked up Jimmy. Enough time to phone Mr. Wainwright. Pushing the *away* button on her phone, Chloe gathered her purse and sweater, then grabbed the laptop. Fingers mentally crossed, she prayed that

Mr. Wainwright would fall in with her plan. Because reading the correspondence had about convinced her it was the only option left.

Viola handed Evan several invoices to approve. "These are going to start flying in now that we have that big order."

Evan didn't look up. "Uh-huh."

"We've all been praying for an answer," Viola continued, "because we're worried about you. Taking everything on yourself the way you do. Well, anyway, everyone's relieved. We had been talking about taking cuts in salary, benefits, whatever it takes to keep things going. Anyway, if we have more going out on this order faster than it comes in, we're willing to make those cuts. And you don't have to wait for the next staff meeting. We've talked about it, so anything you need from us can get done in a New York minute."

Evan stared, unseeing, at the invoices. "It's not the employees' responsibility to prop up the business."

"Pish posh. You're family, Evan. And you've always taken care of us. Don't you think we want to do the same for you?"

His throat clogged. "We have the best people in the world right here at Mitchell Stone."

"And the most diversified."

Emotion was clouding his brain. "Diversified?"

"Like Chloe. Who knew we'd have a former legal secretary doing our filing?"

Legal secretary? Wainwright's legal secretary? Evan searched his mind, trying to remember if he'd seen her name on any of the correspondence. Chloe said she was an estate representative. He frowned. She'd also made that comment about not having the funds to keep her mother at home like he could.

Evan had believed from the beginning that Chloe accepted the assignment strictly for money. But then she'd broken past his initial misgivings, proving to be more than just some moneygrubber. Was he wrong about that, too? Had she been lying to him all this time?

"I really like her," Viola added just before she left.

Shoving aside the invoices, he strode to the file room. Empty. The away button flashed on Chloe's phone. Her desk calendar was askew. Nearing close enough to make out the letters, Evan read her notation. Slowly raising his eyes, he couldn't help wonder. Had Chloe been reporting to Wainwright each day? From Evan's own office?

Disappointment flooded him. And betrayal. But what had he expected? He had betrayed Robin.

Worse, he'd allowed himself to believe.

The wheels were in motion. Chloe had extracted all the information she needed on Mitchell Stone from the records and accounting files. Mr. Wainwright agreed it was a sound proposition and that he would present it to the loan committee. And, since Mr. Wainwright held a lot of sway in the private corporation, the odds of getting the financing were excellent. Her hopes were high, but she hadn't yet told Evan. She feared what might happen if the plan didn't work out.

Now she sat next to Grace in the school auditorium, watching the kids rehearse. Grace's daughter, Susie, was playing a sheep in the scene right after Jimmy's.

He only had a few lines, but Jimmy practiced them over and over each afternoon and evening, wanting to be sure he remembered each and every word on the big night. By now Chloe, along with Thelma, Ned and Gordon, also knew Jimmy's lines since he practiced on all of them. Everyone agreed to come to the performance and Jimmy grew more excited as the play approached.

"Could they be cuter?" Grace asked in a quiet voice, watching her daughter.

"Thanks for keeping an eye on Jimmy. Knowing you're here makes it easier to leave him at school each day."

"I haven't done anything, really. And I intended to help you get settled in. It's sort of a Rosewood tradition."

"I don't know how long I'll be here," Chloe

admitted. "If Evan sticks to his decision, I'll be taking Jimmy back to Milwaukee. Of course, I'm hoping Evan will change his mind." She tried to keep her voice steady. "In any case, I'll be going back."

Grace looked at her searchingly. "Haven't you found a pretty good reason to stay?"

"Am I that transparent?"

"Evan's a good man. It's going to take time, but he'll get past what happened. I don't believe he wants to be alone forever."

Chloe wished it didn't matter so much. "Even if he could... I have to go back and take care of my mother. I'm all she has."

"Families make adjustments all the time."

"Not that kind of adjustment. I don't know if I told you, but when I go back, I'll be attending law school. Marquette, if I can get in there."

"Wow." Grace absently rubbed the scar on her hand. "I didn't picture you pursuing another career. I kind of thought you were ready to tackle raising a family."

Chloe hadn't confided in Grace. She'd promised Mr. Wainwright she would keep his secret, that she would only tell the whole story when it was necessary. Chloe needed a friend, someone to discuss her confused feelings with, but she wasn't accustomed to breaking promises.

The financing matter, however, wasn't a promise. "I did something. And I'm hoping it'll help Evan's business. Now, I'm also hoping he won't be mad since I didn't consult him first."

"It would be easier to give an opinion if I knew what you were talking about."

Chloe outlined the basics. "When I had the idea, I didn't really think about any resentment Evan might have that the money would be coming from Mr. Wainwright's bank. I just wanted to help."

"Evan will no doubt realize that. After all, he helps people all the time. It's in his nature."

"Maybe you're right. I didn't think about it that way."

"I'll pray for you, Chloe, and for Evan and his employees."

Chloe sensed she would need Grace's prayers and all of her own.

Evan stood by the window in his office until he saw Chloe park out front. He waited, giving her time to reach the file room before he walked down the hall. She stood midway between the incoming table and her desk, looking around.

"Expecting more information?"

She whirled around, her brow furrowed.

He took one step inside the now immaculate space. He had removed all of the loose filing, the papers that told the tale of Mitchell Stone's situation.

"What happened? Did Melanie come back?"

"You're good. I'll give you that." Evan walked

closer. "The innocent look, the nearly convincing confusion."

"Apparently not that good. I don't know what you're talking about."

"Haven't you been talking to Wainwright lately?"

The truth flashed across her face. "I was going to explain—"

"That you've been reporting to him ever since you got to town?"

"Well, of course, I've checked in, but—"

"Like a good secretary."

The color drained from her face. "Mr. Wainwright didn't think you'd take me as seriously if—"

"So you've been lying since we met."

Chloe drew in a shaky breath. "I did as Mr. Wainwright instructed. I work for him, yes. As his private secretary. But, when I agreed to bring Jimmy, my position changed."

"To a far more lucrative one?"

Indecision flashed in her clear eyes. "Let me explain—"

"I don't understand why you want all the inside information on the business. That piece doesn't fit. Wainwright can't blackmail me into taking Jimmy."

Chloe looked genuinely appalled. "Blackmail? With what?"

"With whatever you've gathered that you emailed to Wainwright."

Chloe's gaze flickered back to her laptop sitting on the desk. "You went through my personal computer?"

"What are you really doing here, Chloe?"

She blinked. "I thought I was helping." Pain darkened her eyes and she bit down on her lip. "That was my intention. But you're right. Mr. Wainwright did make me an offer that, as they say, I couldn't refuse. If I got you to agree to be Jimmy's guardian, made sure that he was happy here, Mr. Wainwright promised to raise my salary and pay for law school. I wouldn't have to work any longer, but getting paid, I could make it through law school in the normal three years." She pushed the hair off her forehead. "Obviously, I have nothing to do here any longer. I'll leave my laptop so you have enough time to read everything you want. I do need it back, though." Pausing, she took another breath. "And I'll need your final decision about Jimmy."

Before Evan realized her intent, Chloe pushed past him, running down the hall and out the front reception area.

Viola walked up behind him. "Is something wrong?"

Everything. Absolutely everything.

She couldn't breathe. Having no place to run, Chloe had driven to the school, then remained in her rental car. Had she just blown Jimmy's future? Why had she told Evan in such a clinical manner?

Because his words hurt so badly.

Leaning her head against the steering wheel, she felt the tears roll down her face, wetting her shirt. How would she tell Jimmy?

Horrified, another thought hit. What if Evan wanted them gone before Jimmy could play the little shepherd boy?

She'd ruined everything. And, Evan didn't even know the truth. Deep in her heart, Chloe couldn't regret asking Mr. Wainwright to help Evan. It was the right thing to do. But the price was greater than she'd expected.

Someone knocked on her window and she jumped.

Seeing it was Grace, Chloe rolled down the window.

Grace took one look, then opened the door. "Come on."

"But—"

"My kids are in the library for the next hour. Let's get out of here."

Chloe stumbled out of the car and Grace gripped her arm. "My car's right over here." With the kindness of a sister and the sternness of a mother, she got Chloe seated in the car. Leaving the school, she drove to the café on Main Street. "It's quiet this time of day. Most everybody's already eaten breakfast and it's too early for lunch."

"Grace, really, it's not necessary."

"You're the color of a shucked oyster. It's necessary." Grace guided her inside, choosing the farthest booth in the rear. She grabbed a paper napkin from the holder and passed it across the table.

Chloe wiped her cheeks. "I'm not usually this weepy."

"I'm guessing you have good reason."

Biting her lip, Chloe nodded.

"Did Evan overreact?"

"In a way." Chloe repeated her exchange with Evan. "I didn't even get to tell him why I was calling Mr. Wainwright." Her voice started to shake. "But when he accused me of blackmail..."

A waitress approached. "Two hot teas, strong please."

The woman disappeared and Chloe tried to pull herself together. "And I didn't explain why the money's so important." She told Grace about her mother's illness, the cost of the care facility.

Grace leaned forward. "Tell me more."

And Chloe did, detailing her financial situation. "I can't believe I acted so stupidly. I thought about myself instead of Jimmy. I was indignant for both of us, but I could have handled it better, not alienated Evan. Oh, Grace, what if Evan makes us leave before Jimmy's play?"

Grace covered Chloe's hand with her own. "Evan is not an unkind man. You've seen how he protects the people he cares about. He wouldn't deliberately hurt Jimmy. He may not have thought about the play in the last few days, but he can't forget about it completely. He got corralled into moving the boulder during the performance."

"I don't think reminding him about that will improve his mood."

Grace smiled gently. "There are a lot of reasons for having friends."

"Yes."

"One of them is to divert the knight so you can slay the dragon."

Chloe blinked.

The waitress brought the tea, caught Grace's expression and disappeared.

"Let me talk to him first," Grace explained. "Right now you're both raw, in pain. I'm not. I won't fall apart if Evan loses his temper, says something he'll regret. And I won't hold it against him." She picked up her cup. "Now, drink your tea while it's hot."

Chloe reached for her cup. "You never impressed me as being the bossy sort."

"Only with people I care about." Grace sipped her tea. "I'm going to need this. Dragons can be scary."

At the end of the work day, Evan sat in his office. Chloe hadn't returned. Hadn't called. He sighed, mentally going over her words for at least the hundredth time. Hearing a soft knock, he looked up.

"Evan?" Grace Brady stood in the doorway.

He stood. "Come in."

"Do you have a minute?"

"Sure."

She sat in the chair opposite his and folded her hands. "I know it's been a rough day."

Evan lifted his eyebrows. *She did?*

"And I'd like to talk to you about Chloe."

Instinctively he stiffened, his defenses kicking in.

"When Chloe told you about Mr. Wainwright's offer today, she didn't tell you why she accepted."

"It's pretty obvious."

"You'd think so, wouldn't you?" Grace's gentle manner was deceptively unnerving. "But did you question why Chloe needed the money so badly?"

"Same reason everyone wants money, I suppose."

Grace leaned forward. "She's not like everyone. And she doesn't want the money—she *needs* it. Has Chloe told you about her mother?"

Evan frowned. "She's in a nursing home."

"No. She's in an extended-care facility because she has severe chronic pulmonary disease and can't be on her own."

"Okay."

"Have you thought about how Chloe pays for the home?"

"I assume she's paid well."

"Not that well. It takes every penny she makes to pay the facility and their rates are constantly rising. Evan, Chloe lives in a cheap one-room efficiency because she refuses to allow her mother to be placed in a state-run facility. Chloe's out of choices. Mr. Wainwright's offer is the only option she has. Her father's dead. Her younger brother barely makes enough in the military to support his young family. So, her mother's care is completely on Chloe's shoulders."

Evan listened.

Grace met his gaze, her own imploring. "What would you do? What if you were the only one Gordon had to count on?"

"That doesn't explain why she's passing on all our financial information to Wainwright."

"No." Grace unfolded her hands. "It doesn't."

When she didn't say more, Evan prompted her. "So?"

"I'll leave that for her to tell. When Chloe wondered about you, we, all your friends, surrounded you with a wall of protection. Now, Chloe deserves the same wall."

"Because she has something to hide?"

"Did *you* have something to hide?"

He didn't reply.

"Of course not. Evan, consider the woman you've grown to know. Does she have any of the qualities you think you've discovered? Is she uncaring? Selfish? Does Jimmy mean nothing to her?" Grace rose. "I know you have a lot to think about and I'll leave you to it. Just remember, you're not the only one who's hurting. And certainly not the only one who'll be hurt if you do something rash."

An image of Jimmy's eager face flashed in Evan's mind. As quickly, he thought of Sean, how he would have done anything to spare him pain.

But what was Chloe hiding? And why did her deceit cut so deep?

Chapter Thirteen

Tied in knots, Chloe waited for the other shoe to drop. That night at dinner she sat next to Jimmy, ready to protect him if there was an outburst from Evan. Gordon looked at her oddly, but didn't say anything. To her relief, Evan didn't make an appearance. She really didn't want to play out the entire scene in front of everyone.

After dinner she read to Jimmy until he was sleepy, then tucked him in, ferociously guarding his room through the night. She didn't even change into her pajamas and robe, wanting to be prepared.

By morning, bleary-eyed, her throat gravelly, she braced herself.

But nothing happened. Again, Evan was absent.

On nervous autopilot, she drove Jimmy to school, then waited until Grace's free period. Digging in her purse, she found Grace's cell number and phoned. They agreed to meet in the empty auditorium.

Watching anxiously, Chloe was relieved to see that Grace was smiling as she slipped into the closest seat.

Grace's concern filled her face. "How are you holding up?"

"I guess I'm not really sure. I haven't seen Evan since the... since we talked yesterday."

"I'm not surprised."

Chloe's brow furrowed. "Really?"

Grace searched her eyes. "In spite of what happened yesterday, you know what kind of man Evan is."

Looking away, Chloe gripped the handle of her purse. "And now he knows what kind of person I am."

"You can't go down that road. If Evan understands anything, it's family. Your reasons for taking on this job are honorable. And, I've seen how you are with Jimmy. He's not an assignment anymore—you care for him like a mother."

"This is so silly," Chloe wiped away the sudden tears. "I haven't cried this much in years. Now I'm the Trevi fountain."

"Love does that to a person."

"I do love Jimmy," she admitted.

"Just Jimmy?"

Chloe met Grace's steady gaze. "I'm certainly not the kind of woman Evan wants in his life."

"You're so sure?"

"I told you before. Even if he did, I have to go home. Besides, right now I'm the last person in the world Evan wants to see."

Grace remained quiet a few moments. "I'm guessing you don't want to go back to his office to help out anymore."

"The welcome sign's been removed."

"Would you like to volunteer here? The younger grades can always use adults to help with reading, that sort of thing. Or in the library—even grading papers would be appreciated."

Chloe thought about it. "I do need to stay busy."

"Let's get some coffee in the teacher's break room, then why don't you stick with me today?"

Glad for the reprieve, Chloe agreed. "Oh, Grace. Was Evan furious when he found out why I'd contacted Mr. Wainwright?"

"Guess you'll find out when you decide to tell him."

"You didn't?"

"He needs to hear it from you. I just told Evan that he had the wrong idea about the money Mr. Wainwright offered to pay you."

Absorbing her words, Chloe rose, following Grace from the auditorium. So, she still had to face Evan. Something told her he wouldn't be any happier about the second portion of her news than he'd been about the first.

* * *

In the spring, Lark's meadow was a stunning mix of bluebonnets, bright orange paintbrush and golden coreopsis. Now it stood fallow, the wildflowers tuckered down for the winter, the grass withered, yellowing. Yet, to Evan's way of thinking, it was still beautiful in a different way, standing solid, nestling the seeds of the perennial flowers. It was in its keeping mode. Just as he was.

Evan looked upward, into the sky, searching the heavens. It had been so long since he'd whispered a prayer or even believed God was listening. Yet, now his heart told him he needed to try, to seek the light in his darkness. "I still don't understand about Robin and Sean. But this time I'm not asking for me. Lord, these are good people and they need Your help. There aren't other jobs for them to get. You know that. And You know that the older ones will be the worst off. I've poured everything I've got into keeping the place alive and I won't be able to help them. But You can. At least that's what I always believed." Evan felt his throat working and he paused. "I'll accept whatever direction You guide us in." Again he had to stop, to fight against the shaking in his chest. "And, I'll try to understand why You took my boy so soon." Evan bent his head as he appealed to the Lord's gift of grace. Around him, the wind whistled, picking up faded petals, scattering them upward and away. Taking his plea, Evan prayed silently. And bringing back hope.

Chloe kept busy between volunteering at school in a few classes, and with the Christmas play.

Then she helped Thelma prepare and deliver numerous Christmas baskets. No one was overlooked. Shut-ins, the people from Thanksgiving dinner, others on their own, aging couples, and some large families. In addition, a basket was prepared for each employee and his or her family. Chloe felt the most emotion when they reached Melanie's house. The woman threw her arms around Chloe in a spontaneous hug, thanking her for keeping her job available. Proudly, Melanie showed her the new baby who happily kicked his chubby legs in greeting.

Now, the play wasn't far away. It was held in the week school let out for Christmas break, giving families time to gather.

And they were gathering. Chloe had seen some unfamiliar faces in the stores recently, Rosewood descendants who had moved away, but returned to celebrate with their families. If Rosewood were her home, Chloe mused, she would never leave. It had everything. All except one very important person, her mother.

In numerous phone calls, her mother assured

Chloe that Christmas was celebrated fully at the care facility, that old friends might visit, that she would be completely all right. But Chloe couldn't stop worrying.

Combined with waiting for Evan's confrontation, she was on edge when her cell phone rang. Seeing that it was Mr. Wainwright's private number, Chloe answered on the first ring.

"Mitchell's loan has been approved," he began without wasting time on small talk.

Relief flooded her. "That's wonderful. Thank you, Mr. Wainwright."

"What about Jimmy? Has Mitchell made his decision?"

Chloe bit down on her lip. *Not officially.* "Not yet. Mr. Wainwright, if he does say no, will the loan be withdrawn?"

"No. I won't blackmail the man. And Jimmy certainly wouldn't have a happy home under the circumstances."

She closed her eyes, remembering Evan using that same awful word. *Blackmail.* "Thank you."

"Let me know as soon as you can about Jimmy."

Agreeing, she bid her boss goodbye.

Now she just had to tell Evan.

Evan stared at the pile of envelopes stacked neatly on his desk. Christmas bonuses. Each and every employee had returned what most certainly could be their last bonus. Their sacrifice touched him greatly. While they were all paid well, each could use the money to provide Christmas for their families.

Hearing a stir in the hall, Evan glanced up. Chloe stood hesitantly in his doorway.

He rose, staring while she reached his desk and faced him. Belatedly, his voice returned. "Sit down."

She did, perching on the edge of the chair. "I suppose you wonder why I'm here."

Evan sank down into his own chair, wondering that and so much more.

"I want to explain why I collected the information about Mitchell Stone." Chloe swallowed visibly. "When you told me that the financing fell through and that you didn't believe you could secure it anywhere else, I had an idea." Glancing down, she took a deep breath. "I remembered that one of our clients at the law firm is a privately owned bank and that Mr. Wainwright is a member of the board there. After I got all the data together, I called him and asked if he thought the bank might finance your deal." She heard Evan's sharp intake of breath but didn't dare stop. "He agreed to present it to the loan committee. And…" She took a deep breath. "I heard back from Mr. Wainwright. The loan's approved. You have your financing. No strings attached."

You have your financing.

Lord, can this be so?

Chloe scooted forward another inch or so. "As I said, no strings attached. The loan isn't dependent on your answer about Jimmy. Mr. Wainwright...and I...know that wouldn't only be unfair, it wouldn't be in Jimmy's best interest."

Evan tried to collect his thoughts. "Are you sure you told him how large a loan we need?"

"I confirmed it with Perry.... Mr. Perkin."

"Perry didn't say anything."

"I didn't tell him why I needed to know," she admitted. "I didn't want to raise any false hopes, just in case...." Chloe opened her purse and pulled out an envelope. "Mr. Wainwright had the loan package faxed to me. The contact person and phone number at the bank are on the cover letter."

For once in his life, Evan could not think of a single thing to say. Chloe had just presented him with the means to save his business, his employees. And, the first time he had prayed since the accident, the Lord had answered loud and clear. He had forgiven Evan's railings, blame, accusations of betrayal. In His grace, He had taken care of His children.

It was too much to take in at once.

"Well, then." Chloe stood. "I have to get back to

the school. I'm helping out with the rehearsals for the Christmas play."

She reached the doorway before he found his voice. "Chloe."

Pausing, she turned back to face him.

"You don't know what this means."

Her eyes darkened and a surprisingly sad smile tipped her lips upward slightly. "I think I do." Spinning around, she hurried out of his office.

Evan watched even when he couldn't see her any longer. Still mesmerized, his gaze fell on the neat envelope sitting on his desk. Emotions crowded faster than shoppers at a discount sale. Why hadn't she told him when he first confronted her?

If Grace hadn't explained the reason Chloe had been so desperate for money, he *still* wouldn't know about her sacrifices. As the impact continued reverberating, Evan picked up his phone, knowing there was one thing he could do.

A few nights later, Chloe was surprised when Evan appeared for dinner, his mood calm. Jimmy chattered at him, pleased that he was there.

After they ate, Chloe expected Evan to disappear into his study. Instead, he accompanied them into the den while Jimmy told him every tiny detail about the play.

"And Susie Brady's gonna be the lamb. But *I* get to sit on the big rock. I'm the only one who does in the *whole* play."

"I'm the one who gets to move that boulder," Evan reminded him.

"So you'll be there?" Jimmy asked excitedly, his eyes lighting up.

"Of course. Would I miss seeing you play the shepherd boy?"

Chloe nearly dropped her cup of cider. Perhaps her imagination had run amuck. Evan couldn't have actually said he was attending the play.

Jimmy bounced in his chair. "Do you want to see my costume?"

Inwardly Chloe groaned. She had hoped to herd Jimmy upstairs before he latched on to Evan.

"Sure." Evan leaned back in his chair.

Jimmy ran from the room, his sneakers hitting the stairs in rapid succession.

Immediately, Chloe felt the pressure of Evan's gaze. She hadn't been alone with him since the day in his office when she'd told him about the loan. Since then she rationalized that he wouldn't choose that particular time to get into the subject of her deception. Not when he'd been presented the critical financing on a platter. But nothing was stopping Evan now. *Except possibly his father.*

Gordon emptied his pipe, then placed it in his lips without adding any tobacco.

"Running low on tobacco, Dad?"

"Just need it for thinking."

"Anything in particular?"

Gordon hesitated, then glanced up at the portraits lining the mahogany walls. "Just missing your mother."

Chloe sighed. She certainly was missing hers.

"Chloe?" Evan asked.

She jumped. Embarrassed by the reaction, she felt her cheeks flushing. "Yes?"

"Does Jimmy need help with his costume?"

"Just with the head covering and belt. The staff he'll carry that night is stored at school."

Only minutes later, Jimmy pounded down the stairs. As Chloe predicted, he wore the one piece shepherd's robe and carried the accessories. He ran straight to her for help.

Smiling, she adjusted his cotton hat and tied the rope that served as a belt. Then she winked. "All set."

He grinned and turned to Evan. "I get to carry this stick thing while I talk."

"Do you know all your lines?"

"I should say so," Gordon replied for him. "He's practiced all afternoon, every afternoon, since he got the part."

Evan's expression grew reflective, almost nostalgic.

Chloe guessed he was missing his son.

"And everybody's coming to see me," Jimmy declared. "Thelma's gonna make a special cake."

"Sounds good. Thelma makes the best cakes in town. Maybe the world."

"It's gonna be chocolate and have lots of frosting. Thelma said," J–immy confided.

Looking at and listening to the child she had come to love as her own, Chloe hoped the night of the play wouldn't be the last that she and Jimmy stayed in this house. Or the last they were together.

Chapter Fourteen

"It's bona fide." Perry plopped the financing contract on Evan's desk.

"Legal opinion?" Evan asked.

"Combed through word by word. It's solid. No balloon payment, no prepayment penalty. The terms are better than the deal that fell through." Perry studied his friend. "I don't know how Chloe pulled this off, but it's a gift straight from heaven."

Took the words right out of his mouth.

Perry looked at him. "Do you want to give the official go-ahead?"

Evan expelled a deep breath, then shook his head. "I thought our next official statement was going to be…"

"I know." Perry thumped the edge of the desk with his fist. "Probably isn't the best time to say this, but I've been thinking it a while now, so I might as well.

The day Chloe and Jimmy showed up on your front porch was a gift, too."

Evan swivelled in his desk chair. "It's complicated."

"Ouch."

Turning back to Perry, Evan frowned. "What's that supposed to mean?"

"It's a cop-out. Life *is* complicated. You know that better than most people." Perry narrowed his gaze. "Are you really going to let her slip away?"

"How do you know she's interested?"

"Unlike you, I'm not blind." Perry shook his head in two rapid nods of disbelief.

"Message received."

"Same message—part two. Don't waste any more time."

Evan couldn't keep the sardonic tone from his voice. "That all?"

"I'm sure I can think of plenty more."

"Do me a favor."

Perry grinned. "Stop thinking?"

"Nah. Keep reminding me."

The night of the play was clear and cool. Although snow wouldn't blanket the hill country town, it hadn't blanketed Bethlehem either. Parents, siblings, students and interested community members filled the school auditorium.

Evan was backstage, waiting until it was time

to move the boulder. And, ridiculously, he felt nervous. What if Jimmy forgot his lines? What if he got scared? Didn't want to go on? The teacher had the children lined up in groups, in order of appearance. So it was difficult to talk to him with the other kids around. And Jimmy was one of the last to go on.

As the play began, the older kids did well. Some kindergartners and first graders froze, a few cried. And Evan's nerves accelerated. Then it was time for him to move the boulder. The lights dimmed, the curtain closed and Evan quickly crossed the stage, lifting the large rock to the center.

A few parents, waiting to reassure their children, crowded into the space where he'd been waiting. The side drape blocked the stage while Evan found a new spot. When the main curtain rose, Jimmy sat on the boulder, alone. Evan sucked in his breath, mentally reassuring Jimmy that he would be all right.

The large star, constructed by the high school art department, hung at the highest point. It lit up suddenly, eliciting murmurs of admiration from the audience.

Jimmy stood, the curved staff by his side. Gazing up at the shining piece of scenery, Jimmy's face was radiant. Then the words he'd so diligently practiced poured out. "Papa! Papa! Do you see the star?"

Frozen with pride, a surge of love overwhelmed Evan, amazing him. He didn't think he had that much love left in him. Evan thought he'd given all of it to

Sean and Robin. But his heart expanded, telling him there was room for Jimmy. Mindless of anyone who might see, he let the tears fill his eyes.

Blind. Perry was right. He hadn't seen what was in front of him. None of it.

Someone gasped near him. Evan didn't want to tear his eyes from Jimmy, but shifted slightly, just in time to see Chloe withdrawing her hand, then quickly walking away. Had she been about to comfort him? Did she care that much?

A group of children crowded close, ready to go on next. Evan had to move so they could get past him. In the confusion, he missed seeing Jimmy as he left the stage. Several older high school boys carried scenery, blocking the exits.

Evan waited, then finally eased out the back door. It didn't take too long to circle the school, then come back in through the front. The play had ended and the crowd was breaking up, some pausing to chat, others waiting for their children.

Dodging small groups, he made his way to where he had seen Chloe sitting. Gordon, Thelma and Ned visited with the Markhams. Jimmy ran from the stage to Chloe. She knelt, giving him a huge hug. Getting closer, he could hear her praising his performance.
. "You were the very best one!"

He bounced on his dark sneakers. "Really?"

"Really!" She hugged him again. "The very, very, very best."

Jimmy hugged her back hard before finally letting go.

"You haven't told me what you want for Christmas yet, big guy."

"A family."

She leaned her head against his, caramel and dark twined together. "Me, too."

Evan stopped, struck by their words. The star on the stage twinkled, beaconing its message of hope. And he wondered if he dared believe.

Hanging the phone up slowly, Evan sank back in his chair. The normally comforting feel of the den didn't help. Jimmy's grandparents in Egypt were ready to step up and take guardianship. They planned to enroll him in the same school Spencer had loathed. They hoped to spend some holidays with Jimmy. Just as they had intended to with Spencer.

Cousin Spencer had always been so excited when he got to Rosewood. And the night before he returned to school he always cried himself to sleep. Years had passed, but the memories had never left. Evan remembered his parents' discussions about Spencer. They had always hoped to convince his parents to let him stay permanently in Rosewood. But they insisted Spencer's education was paramount. His feelings hadn't been.

Evan's throat closed, imagining Jimmy crying himself to sleep, longing for a family. The family he was wishing for right now. The family Chloe wanted.

Now he had to tell her what Jimmy's grandparents wanted. Pushing his own want aside, Evan couldn't help wondering if family would be the deciding factor. Or, if Wainwright's offer would win out in the end.

Sitting at the kitchen table, Chloe carefully cut some beautiful burgundy foil paper. She and her mother had always made gift wrapping an event, finding the most unusual papers, creating beautiful ornaments to place on the packages. Then hot cocoa and cookies.

This year, Christmas was going to be a post office event. She'd mailed her mother's presents. The home's director had repeatedly assured her there would be a celebration that day. Thinking of it, Chloe wanted to cry.

Her brother couldn't help. Chip apologized, but there was no way he could afford the trip. Just sending a gift had strained their tight budget.

Jimmy ran into the kitchen, Bailey on his heels. "Ned said I could help him in the shed if you say it's okay."

"Sure. Be careful and mind Ned."

He skipped out the back door in seconds.

Chloe hoped Ned would like the gloves she'd bought for him. They were a quality leather pair that he could wear to church. She fitted the paper beneath a box. Hearing the door from the dining room open, she was glad the gloves were hidden. She liked all of the presents to be a surprise for everyone. It had been a family tradition. "If you need the table, Thelma, I'll be done in a jiff."

"I don't need the table," Evan replied.

Surprised, she glanced up at him. "I just assumed—"

"Jimmy's grandparents called."

The blood seemed to drain from her entire body. Hands slack, she dropped the scissors.

Evan ignored them. "They're ready to take guardianship."

Appalled, Chloe stared.

"Unless I do," Evan finished. He walked to the window, staring out back. No doubt Jimmy and Bailey were in sight.

"Are they coming back? To the states?"

"Only long enough to enroll Jimmy in school. Seems they have to meet with the university board about the grant for their dig. So, they can kill two birds with one stone. Direct quote."

Chloe thought she was going to be sick. "What did you tell them?"

"They're going to call after Christmas, confirm their plans."

So Evan hadn't refused, hadn't said he was going to accept the guardianship.

"What do you think Wainwright will say?"

Chloe jerked her face up, unable to believe what she was hearing. "Wainwright?" Truly sickened, she jumped up. "So that's what's bothering you? You think Mr. Wainwright will pull your financing if Jimmy's grandparents take him?" Holding back her tears, Chloe ran from the kitchen, up the stairs and into her room. *Her* room. A guest room in a house she had hoped would be Jimmy's home. Disappointment in Evan cut to the bone. She had been praying that he would grow to love Jimmy. Perhaps she should have prayed for him to get a heart.

Evan looked over the quarry's last safety inspection. Everything had been up to standard. But with the huge order to work on, he didn't want to wait another month to conduct the next one. With Christmas only two days away, a few office employees had taken off, but most of the quarry workers were in place.

"I thought this new deal had stone coming out of most all of Mitchell's quarries," Dilbert Dunn, their longtime stone mason, commented.

"It will. But every site has to be checked."

"Not due yet."

"Better early than late. I'm not compromising anyone's safety," Evan insisted.

"You're the boss, but it could wait until after Christmas."

Decisions. Everyone wanted him to make decisions. As though they were as easy to make as flipping a coin. "You can leave, Dilbert. There are enough guys here to manage."

"Haven't missed a safety test yet. Not going to miss this one."

If Evan had a smile anywhere in him, he would have grinned. But there wasn't an ounce of humor to be found. Chloe's accusation rang in his ears. And, if she was that quick to accuse him, she couldn't possibly feel the way he'd hoped.

Dilbert plucked a clipboard from a peg on the wall of the utilitarian office. "Better run a check on who clocked in today."

While Dilbert compared time cards to his list, Evan stared off toward the dusty limestone pit. Only two days until Christmas. And then he had to face Jimmy's grandparents alone. Because Chloe would be packing for home.

Chloe sat in the porch swing, remembering her one evening with Evan on this same porch, wondering how she could have been so wrong about him. She thought she had seen tenderness, understanding and kindness in him. Was it an illusion? Worse, a delusion of her own making? Had she infused him with characteristics he didn't possess?

A vision of him on the night of the school play flashed in her thoughts. She hadn't imagined the openly raw emotions as he watched Jimmy, nor the tears. Seeing how deeply he was affected, Chloe had wanted to comfort him, even reached out a hand to do so. But, knowing how private Evan was about his feelings, she stopped at the last moment.

Who was Evan? The man who was moved to tears watching an orphan play a shepherd boy? Or the one who coldly announced that Jimmy's grandparents were going to claim him?

The back door creaked as it opened and Gordon stepped out. "Well, hello there. I thought I was the only one who liked to sit outside in the winter."

She dredged up a faint smile. "Cool air can be bracing."

He looked at her more closely. "That was said like you need it."

Chloe shook her head, not wanting to worry the older man. He had consistently been kind to her since they met. Thoughtful and caring, his concern for Jimmy was genuine.

"Mind if I join you?" Gordon asked.

She scooted over to one side so he had room to sit. "Of course not."

The swing creaked as he sank down. "This old swing's a great place to think." He chuckled. "And watch the kids. Evan was a pistol. And he always had friends around, enough to be more than a handful to keep under control." They rocked quietly for a while, then Gordon continued, "We wanted more children, but weren't blessed with another. Evan had so many friends, it seemed like he didn't miss having siblings. Now, I wonder."

"I don't see my younger brother often anymore. Now that Chip has children, his family's his focus."

"That was Evan—the family man," Gordon explained. "When Sean was born, everything clicked in place for him. It was the role Evan had been waiting for all his life. That's when he expanded the business, the legacy for Sean. Oh, that's not why the company's in trouble now. The economy's responsible for the business problems." He paused, glancing out over the immaculate yard. All the fallen leaves had been raked into piles, then burned in an old steel drum barrel. The climbing roses, now bare of beautiful blossoms, rustled in the light breeze. "Hope this wind doesn't pick up."

"I've prayed that Evan might come to care for Jimmy," Chloe confessed. She couldn't bear the thought of him being hurt. Closing her eyes, she pictured the confusion and betrayal in Jimmy's face when she told him they would be leaving, that he would be living in a boarding school.

"And you don't think Evan does?" Gordon furrowed his brow, studying her closer. "Can't you see it? The way he watches Jimmy when he thinks no one can see him? The longing to let go of the past, take a chance? The fear that if he does, something will happen to Jimmy. Evan puts on the mask of being tough, caring only about business, but you have to know by now that's not all there is to my son."

Chloe bent her face down, thinking of all the people at Thanksgiving dinner, people whose lives Evan had touched, improved, cared about. "Then why is he willing to let Jimmy go to Spencer's parents?"

Shocked, Gordon scrunched his eyebrows down. "That can't be true."

The wind increased, ruffling her hair. "They called yesterday, told Evan they're ready to accept guardianship. They plan to enroll him in boarding school."

"Like Spencer?" Gordon asked, appalled.

"Exactly."

"Now that they're older, maybe they plan to return to the states, be closer to him."

Chloe emphatically shook her head. "That's just it! They plan to stay on the dig. Oh, and they hope to spend a few holidays with Jimmy."

"You've got to be wrong about this," Gordon objected. "I know Evan. He wouldn't do that to the child. He may be afraid to voice his love since he lost Sean, but, if anything, he's more empathic than ever with kids."

She sighed, wishing that were true. "He's more worried about what Mr. Wainwright might do about the financing than he is about Jimmy's grandparents."

Gordon looked confused.

"Did Evan tell you that the original loan for the company's big new order fell through?"

"No."

"He probably didn't want to worry you. Anyway, I had the idea of hooking him up with my boss. Mr. Wainwright sits on the board of a privately owned bank. Mitchell Stone got the loan it needs through him. It's enough to save the company. Now, that's all Evan cares about."

"Was the guardianship issue a provision of getting the loan?"

"Well, no." Chloe bit down on her lower lip. "Actually, there aren't any strings attached. It's a straight-out business loan with good terms."

"Then his consideration of what Wainwright thinks can't be motivating Evan." Gordon frowned. "Are you sure it's not a little closer to home than that?"

Now, Chloe was confused. "What do you mean?"

"My, you really haven't been paying attention. Jimmy isn't the only person Evan studies when he thinks no one's watching."

Chloe blinked.

And Gordon chuckled. "Evan can't keep his eyes off of you."

"But he's always so gruff!"

"You know Evan. Would you expect him to show up with flowers and chocolates?"

Not really. Especially in his own house. "Still, Gordon, I think that's wishful thinking."

"You haven't done any of your own?"

She had indulged in too many thoughts of how it would be to have Evan as her husband, Jimmy as her son. But that was wishing, not real life. "I have," she admitted. "But mostly for Jimmy. It would kill me to see him shut away in some boarding school. And he worships Evan. They should be together."

"And you?"

Her lips trembled before she got them under control. "My life's complicated. It's also back in Milwaukee with my mother. Besides, I think you and I both must have caught the same wishing bug."

"It's not contagious," Gordon said kindly. "Chloe, do you think your mother would want to be responsible for your unhappiness?"

"Of course not! But—"

He held up one hand. "As parents, what we want more than anything in the world is our children's happiness. That's what makes us happy. And, Chloe, I'm guessing you haven't considered the changes you could make."

Chloe choked up. "I can't make my mother well. And I won't desert her."

Gordon looked as though he wanted to say more.

Instead, he expelled a deep breath, looked out again over the yard and gardens, then frowned. "The wind's a lot stronger."

Her mind still muddled, Chloe pulled her sweater tighter. "Maybe a storm's coming."

"Did Evan tell you what time he's conducting the test?"

"Test?"

"It's a safety inspection. This one's not due yet, but Evan wants to make sure everything's safe before they start on the big order," Gordon explained.

Confused, Chloe looked at him in question. "Does the wind have any bearing?"

"They'll be setting charges. I never like doing that in the wind. It's not supposed to affect the timing or the detonator, but when we do a full-out test, I want clear, calm weather." Gordon checked his watch. "I'm going to call Evan, see when it's planned."

"Will he postpone it if you ask?"

Although Gordon still looked concerned, he smiled encouragingly. "Chloe, he's not perfect, but he's a good son."

Slightly ashamed, she nodded. "Of course. I'm just emotional today." A thought struck her. "What if he's already doing the test?"

"I'll make that call." Gordon disappeared in the house.

Suddenly worried, she followed.

Chloe left so quickly she didn't hear the rustle in the bushes beside the porch or the flash of blue jeans as they disappeared into the shed.

Dilbert glared into the rising dust. "I don't know, Evan. Your dad always wanted clear weather when we tested."

"Are you about done checking the time cards?"

"Considering the weather, I say we double-check. And run a radio check before we start."

Evan sighed. "I've got the time." His mind was full of the distressing call from Jimmy's grandparents and Chloe's unexpected, wounding response.

"You sure Mac said he was taking off?"

Trying to remember, Evan shook his head. "I'll go check with Bud." The foreman always knew exactly who was on duty in case of an accident. "Double-check with the office. Viola will have his vacation slip if he put in for time off." As he walked out of the shed, Evan noticed that the wind had increased since he'd arrived. The dry hill country air couldn't tamp down the dirt and dust from a strong wind. Usually, rain accompanied their storms, alleviating much flying debris.

Evan found Bud checking the detonator. "Is Mac working today?"

"Nah. Took off."

"Dilbert's worrying like an old lady," Evan explained. "He's checked the time cards twice."

Bud rattled off the names of the men who were in the quarry. "Tell him I know what I'm doing."

Dilbert and Bud had an ongoing rivalry that wouldn't end while either was still alive. Luckily, it never got in the way of doing their jobs. "So, we're set?"

"Yep."

Evan thought he heard something. "You hear that?"

Bud shook his head. "Nah. Probably an echo from the canyon."

"Right." Evan realized he was picking up on Dilbert's anxiety. No place for it in his business. And, right now, blowing up the side of a hill suited his mood just fine.

Chapter Fifteen

Gordon pushed Redial again. Again, after a few rings, Evan's cell phone went to voice mail. "He's not picking up."

"And no one's answering at the little office out there?" Chloe asked, her worry escalating.

"The shed just has one line and it's busy. Dilbert always fusses when we've talked about upgrading the place. All the workers have radios, which has worked out fine so far."

Ned knocked on the door frame.

Gordon waved him inside.

"Is it okay for Jimmy to be out riding on that old bike? He tore out of here like his pants were on fire. Now the wind's getting fierce."

Fear hit Chloe harder than any wind could. "When? When did he leave, Ned?"

"Better than half an hour ago. Right after he played that little joke on you."

"Joke?" Gordon asked.

"He hid next to the back porch so he could jump out and surprise you." Ned looked from Gordon to Chloe. "Didn't you see him?"

"No." Chloe stared at Gordon. "But he probably heard us." Trying not to panic, Chloe quickly calculated how long it would take a seven-year-old to bike to the quarry. Not nearly long enough. "Can you keep trying the shed and Evan's cell? I'll go to the quarry." Running, she grabbed her keys from the entry hall table.

She jumped in the rental car and sped off. "Lord," she prayed. "Please keep Jimmy and Evan safe." It was the middle of the day and last-minute shoppers clogged the road. "And let me get there in time."

But time accelerated, zooming as she remained clogged to a crawl in the quagmire of holiday traffic. The entire time she continued to pray, imploring the Lord to watch out for both Mitchells she loved.

Gordon pushed Redial repeatedly, praying for Evan to pick up. Tuned into his family's needs, Evan never ignored a call from home. Gordon's heart stilled. What if something had already happened? *Lord, I know his faith has wavered... please let my boy know You are watching over him. Keep Jimmy safe so that You might deliver him to Evan's arms.*

* * *

The whipping wind dried the sweat from Jimmy's face and arms as he pedaled faster and faster toward the quarry. He couldn't let Evan get blown up like Mommy and Daddy. His tummy felt funny and his chest kept pounding like it might burst.

He hadn't wanted to come so far from his house to live with Evan. But now he liked Evan a whole bunch. And he liked Uncle Gordon and Thelma and Ned. He wanted Chloe to never leave. But she looked sad now. Like she had a bad secret.

Jimmy wanted Evan and Chloe to be happy. His chest pounded. He didn't know why Mommy and Daddy had gone to heaven, but Chloe said they were always watching over him. Maybe they would watch over Evan, too.

Not sure whether they were watching right now, Jimmy pumped the bicycle as hard as he could. The quarry was just around the next bend. He didn't want Evan to go away to heaven.

A car honked behind him. Jimmy didn't turn around. Mommy and Daddy said they were just going to work. Then they never came home. Jimmy pedaled harder, his legs burning. He wanted Evan to always come home to him.

Evan listened while Viola named all the quarry workers who had opted for a vacation day. "Okay,

Vi. Dilbert's uneasy about today's test, so I figured I'd better be sure. Yeah, I know. I don't *have* to do the safety check today." Putting down the landline, Evan shook his head.

"We could wait until after New Year's," Dilbert reminded him. "We'd have a full crew."

"Dilbert, if I didn't know better, I'd think you're trying to spook me."

The older man shrugged. "Just like to listen to my gut."

Evan wavered for a moment. It wouldn't kill him to wait. But he wanted the test over with. Mostly, he wanted to fill the hours. Empty time with nothing to occupy him left his mind open to thoughts best left alone.

What if he hadn't pushed Chloe away? Had told her of his burgeoning feelings? Evan looked upward, vibrantly aware of the Lord's answer to prayer. Through Chloe, the Lord had opened a door Evan would never have tried.

Evan left the shed, Dilbert muttering behind him. The wind didn't bother Evan. He'd always found it exhilarating.

As he walked, Evan wondered if Chloe's response could have been a defensive one. Had she felt as wounded as he did? Even a good woman could lash out under the right circumstances.

Out of sight from the small office shed, Evan

stopped, bending his head. "Lord, I've faltered. I wouldn't humble myself before until I had no choice, when I thought my people would lose everything." Evan's throat worked. "I made a vow to my wife, Lord. And I meant it forever, until I died. Chloe's changed everything, Lord. She doesn't take, she gives. Only I haven't given back. I keep hurting her instead. Lord, is that what I'm meant to do? So that I can remain faithful to Robin? You know she was a good woman. And, I don't think Robin would want me to hurt Chloe. I need Your guidance, Lord. I need to know what I should do about Chloe and Jimmy. He's in my heart for good now. I'm afraid, Lord. What if I lose him, too? I ask for Your help, Lord, to guide me on the right path."

The dust swirled around his boots. Looking slowly up into the sky, Evan noticed that the sky was graying, the clouds darkening. If he was going to get the test done, he'd better hurry.

Chloe couldn't believe it. Since she had arrived in Rosewood, the streets had never been so full. More like lazy country lanes, even the road leading out of town was normally nearly empty. Had the entire world flocked to the tiny hill country town?

Honking, she considered leaving the car, running the rest of the way. But Jimmy could pedal far faster than she could run. *Lord, he's just a little boy. Please don't take him away. I will do everything to make sure he's happy. I will do anything You guide me to do. Just keep him safe, Lord, please.* She wiped away the tears, then pulled around the car blocking hers, speeding ahead. *Please, Lord.*

Gordon dialed Evan's cell number, listening to it ring, hanging up when it reverted to voice mail. *Where was he? And why wasn't he picking up?*

"Thelma! Ned!" he hollered.

Ned came on a run, Thelma only a few feet behind.

Gordon held out both hands. "We need to pray. For Jimmy and Evan, Chloe, too. I'm afraid there's going to be a terrible accident at the quarry."

Thelma clasped his hand, her eyes filling with tears. Ned gripped his other hand. Closing his eyes, Gordon bent his head. "Lord, we beseech you. Our boys, Evan and Jimmy, and our girl, Chloe, are heading into danger. Please keep them safe so that they might be together again under our roof safely in the arms of those who love them." His voice faltered. "Lord, we ask this in the name of Your Son, the one who saves us all."

Slowly unclasping hands, Thelma crumpled against her husband. And Gordon didn't bother to wipe away the tears. All that he loved most was now in the Lord's hands. He could only believe his heavenly Father would protect them.

* * *

The charges were set. Dilbert had triple-checked employees until Evan finally stopped him. "Everyone's accounted for. The weather's only going to get worse. Let's get this done, then knock off, and everyone can go home. This close to Christmas, people have plans."

Dilbert shook his head, sighed loudly, then slumped on to the stool. "You're the boss."

"You act like you haven't been here through dozens of these tests."

"I've had my say," Dunn retorted, muttering under his breath, slamming the clipboard back on its peg.

Evan pushed in the mike button on his radio set. "Bud. It's a go."

The landline rang suddenly, competing with the whistling wind. Dilbert reached out to answer the call.

"Leave it," Evan told him. "If it's important they'll call back." Picking up his hard hat, he set it firmly on his head, gesturing for Dilbert to do the same.

Muttering, Dunn complied.

Evan picked up his binoculars, zooming in first on the explosives, then the detonator. Swinging around, something glinted off to his far left. The sun was hidden by the clouds. Puzzled, Evan focused on the bright spot. Moving the binoculars up, his heart stilled, his face froze. Desperately, he pushed the radio button. "Abort!"

Static buzzed back in reply.

Flinging the binoculars to the floor, Evan ran from the office shed, legs pumping, heart bursting, mind praying. Jimmy jumped off his bicycle, running toward him.

"No!" Evan shouted, running faster than he ever had.

But the wind swept his words away.

And Jimmy ran toward him even faster.

Evan increased his speed, adrenaline kicking in, hurtling him toward his little boy. Barely slowing as he reached Jimmy, Evan scooped him up, pressing Jimmy to his chest and running away from the blast. He nearly cleared the red-marked danger line when the blast shook the ground, echoed to the canyon and back, and flung Evan to the ground. Holding his body over Jimmy's, Evan formed a protective barrier. The strong wind carried some residual bits of debris, but mostly a huge cloud of dust from the blast.

A car screeched to a stop only a few feet from them. Jerking upward, Evan bent to thrust Jimmy from this newest danger.

Chloe pushed open her car door, hitting the ground at a run, tears streaming down her face as she reached for them.

Picking up Jimmy with one hand, he reached with

his other arm to encircle Chloe, pulling them both into his embrace, silently vowing to never let them go. He had asked the Lord for a sign. Had there ever been a clearer one?

Chloe knelt, checking over Jimmy, reassuring herself that he wasn't hurt. Evan pulled her back up, needing to hold on to her, to both of them.

"I thought…." Chloe bit back a sob. "What if you hadn't seen him?"

"I did. That's all that counts." Evan stroked her silky hair, breathing in the clean scent, knowing he would never forget it. Closing his eyes, he silently thanked the Lord, knowing He had saved them.

Jimmy still shook as he hung on to Evan. "I thought you were gonna get blowed up like Mommy and Daddy."

"Oh, sweetie!" Chloe reached for him, but Evan was quicker, picking the child up and holding him close.

"That's not going to happen to me, Jimmy. I'm here now and I'm always going to be here for you. I want you to live with me, be my son."

Jimmy threw his small arms around Evan's strong neck, holding on for all he was worth. Evan held him close, then lifted his face, catching Chloe's gaze. He had made one commitment. Would another be in his reach?

Gasping, Dilbert reached him. "I thought you were all goners for sure!"

"Dilbert, if I decide not to listen to you in the future, just knock me out with my own hard hat."

"I ain't pleased to be right," Dilbert spit out between repeated gasps. "I tried to get Bud on the radio…" He paused for another deep breath. "But it was too late."

Evan clapped the older man's shoulder, seeing how gray he was beneath his leathery tan.

Bud rushed up, one arm grasping Dilbert's. "You all right, you old fool?" For all their bickering, Bud was as pale as Dilbert.

Other quarry workers surrounded them, checking for injuries, most looking shaken, many shocked. All looked relieved when it was certain no one had been hurt.

Humbled by their concern, Evan knew he had much to be thankful for. Meeting Chloe's eyes once more, he realized how very, very much.

Chapter Sixteen

The light in Jimmy's room was dim. Exhausted, he had fallen asleep soon after eating his dinner. Thelma had fussed over him, using the corner of her apron to wipe her red-rimmed eyes while she offered to cook any and everything he might want. Too tired, emotionally and physically, to care, he had agreed to a bowl of chicken and dumplings. But he didn't eat much, instead leaning against Evan for a while, then Chloe.

Evan had helped Jimmy with his bath, then sat with him while he settled in for the night. Evan continued hovering until he was absolutely certain Jimmy was asleep and content.

Chloe had given Evan space, knowing he needed to reassure himself that Jimmy was really, truly out of danger, that he was safely ensconced beneath the Mitchells' roof. Evan was reluctant to leave, finally forcing himself to go.

Now, Chloe watched as Jimmy slept. Although she had tucked Elbert at his side, Jimmy hadn't reached for him as he usually did. Having an actual human to count on had relieved some of his fear, perhaps all of it. She stroked his dark hair, memorizing each feature, holding fast to this memory.

Stars filled the windswept sky. The storm had moved on, after bringing a light rain to wash the last of the dust away. A fresh start, Chloe mused. Utterly, inescapably grateful for Jimmy's safety, she thought she saw one of the stars blink. *Thank You, Lord, for everything, for keeping them both safe, for opening Evan's heart.*

The star twinkled and Chloe's throat closed. Evan's heart had opened for Jimmy and she was more grateful than she could have ever thought possible. Now that Jimmy had a guardian, one who loved him, her precious child would no longer need her. It was what she wanted, what she had brought Jimmy to Rosewood to find. Although she had told herself it would be difficult to say goodbye, Chloe hadn't imagined the loss now swamping her.

Jimmy would also have Gordon, Thelma and Ned, who clearly loved him as well. And Rosewood was a wonderful place for any child to grow up in. He had caring teachers, friends at school, an inspiring church and caring church family. Now that Evan had committed himself to being Jimmy's guardian, he wouldn't hold back. As in everything, Evan would be on full throttle, ensuring that Jimmy would be an incredibly happy child.

Heart brimming with love, Chloe glanced down at him, sleeping so soundly, so peacefully. This sweet boy would never cry himself to sleep because he was lonely, and all his holidays would be filled with family and tradition. The kind of tradition she had secretly dreamed of, imagining the years stringing out before them like a sparkling garland on the tallest Christmas tree.

The door to Jimmy's room eased open. Thelma stuck in her head, followed by Ned, peering over her shoulder. "Is he okay?" Thelma mouthed soundlessly.

Chloe nodded.

Both smiled back, then left as silently as they had come.

Yes, Jimmy would be encased in more than enough love for one small child. But, he would also be loved from afar because Chloe knew she would always carry him in her heart. This, her first, most precious child.

Jimmy slept deeply, unaware that she watched over him, memorizing the shape of his small nose, the way his eyebrows scrunched together when he was concentrating, the bright light of his soul that shone in his winsome eyes. Gently, she stroked his dark hair again, hoping to leave the tiniest imprint in his consciousness so he wouldn't completely forget her.

Gordon opened the door, crossing silently to the bed. "You won't get a minute's sleep with all of us checking on him," he whispered.

Unable to speak, she stepped back, allowing him access. Gordon would be a wonderful grandfather—loving, caring and fun. It was the best ready-made family she could have hoped for.

"I'll get out of your way," Gordon whispered, patting her back. "Our boy's just fine."

Chloe managed to keep a neutral expression until he left. Then she sank in to the wood rocking chair adjacent to the bed. Earlier, she had moved the chair from its usual spot in the corner so she could sit by Jimmy.

Bending her head she prayed silently. *Dear Lord, please help me show Jimmy that I know he's in the right place. Give me strength. Don't let me show my sadness, my need to stay close. I want what's best for him. But I'll need help, Lord. More help than I've ever needed before.*

Christmas Eve dawned bright, filled with people, noise and mysterious but enticing aromas from the kitchen. Refreshed by a full night of sleep, Jimmy bounced up, ready to tackle another day.

He ran through the open door to Chloe's room. "Chloe! Chloe!"

She turned to him with a smile, determined not to allow her sleepless night and anguish show. "Hey, big guy!"

"I got it already! My family!"

"Yes, you did! I'm so happy for you, Jimmy." So happy that she wanted to die, knowing he and Evan would never be hers.

"And you!" he responded, grinning.

"Me?"

"Sure. Now we're all a family." Jimmy grabbed her neck, his thin arms hugging hard.

Don't cry. Don't cry!

He pulled back. "Can we go see the outside Jesus?"

She mentally translated. "The live nativity?"

"Uh-huh. Uncle Gordon said they'll be there as soon as it's dark. And that it gets dark faster now. Please!"

"Unless Evan has something else planned, I think he'll agree."

"They have a *real* donkey and a lamb. Not like Susie Brady playing the lamb in our play."

Chloe smiled. "That's great. But you know the animals aren't the most important part, right?"

"It's the birthday for Jesus. He was borned where my star is."

"So, what else do you want to do today?"

"Evan's taking me to the store." Jimmy stopped. "It's kind of a surprise."

"Christmas is full of surprises." She pushed a bit of hair from his forehead. "Good surprises. You have fun today, okay?"

"Okay." He bounced on his sneakers, ready to start.

Chloe wasn't sure if she could hold her smile in place any longer. "Head on downstairs. I'll see you a little later."

"Thelma made French toast."

"Sounds delicious."

Jimmy skipped through the doorway, then quickened his pace down the hall to the staircase, finally pounding down the stairs.

Chloe heard voices and the closing of the front door. Moving to her window, she edged the curtain back, seeing Evan and Jimmy walk to the truck. Evan had his arm draped around Jimmy's shoulders. They were a perfect match, as she had known they would be.

Watching until the truck was out of sight, she turned around, looking at the shelf in her open closet where her suitcase was stowed. Although she had more presents to wrap, Chloe wanted to pack while Jimmy was out. He didn't need to watch the process. It was going to be hard enough to say goodbye. When she did, Chloe wanted to be set to flee to her car, to make the break as painless as possible for Jimmy.

Grabbing the empty bag, she laid it on the bed, then opened it. Originally thinking her visit would most likely last only a few weeks, there wasn't too much to gather. Pulling open a dresser drawer, she lifted out the jeans and shirt she'd bought for the hayride. She thought of Evan's kiss, the regret that pained him. Holding the items close, she remembered the sweet smell of fresh hay, the laughter, the moonlight, the feelings Evan had brought to life.

Before she could collapse in tears, she shoved both pieces into the suitcase. Folding the rest of her clothes, Chloe dropped them inside, not caring what wrinkled, not caring if the stuff even made it back to Milwaukee. She left out her nicest dress for Christmas Day.

Although she tried, Chloe couldn't get a reservation out for either Christmas Eve or day. She could at least have spent the holiday with her mother. Thinking of Mom alone was worrying Chloe more and more. And she needed to be gone. To allow Evan and Jimmy to bond, to begin their new relationship. Booking one of the few seats left out of San Antonio for the twenty-sixth, she would remain in Rosewood as shortly as possible.

Chloe opened another dresser drawer, withdrawing the last of her gifts for wrapping. Realizing the paper and other supplies were still in the storeroom off the kitchen, she gathered her strength, and tried to squelch her feelings.

Downstairs, she hesitantly pushed open the swinging door to the kitchen. Smelling the French toast Thelma had mentioned, she spotted a note on the table: *"French toast and bacon in the warming drawer. Syrup's on the counter. Make your own coffee."*

Chloe smiled faintly. The note didn't need a signature. Reading it was like having Thelma standing there, speaking. Having no appetite, Chloe put her gifts down on the table and took Thelma's advice, making a fresh pot of coffee.

Back in the storeroom, the paper had been orderly returned to the shelf. Chloe didn't need much to wrap the few remaining gifts. A lace handkerchief for Thelma, a freshly sealed package of cherry pipe tobacco for Gordon, a children's bible for Jimmy that she had inscribed to him, and a paperweight for Evan, made from his own quarry's limestone. Viola and Dilbert had helped her retrieve the small piece she needed. Dilbert had volunteered to cut the stone for her, then inscribe Evan's initials. Chloe's fingers lingered over the paperweight, then traced the lettering on Jimmy's bible.

"Thought I smelled fresh coffee," Gordon declared as he pushed open the swinging door to the kitchen, sniffing in pleasure. "Thelma always leaves me to my own devices until supper on Christmas Eve.

Personally, I think she turns into one of the elves while she's out." He filled a mug. "Did you get some?"

Chloe shook her head, afraid to trust her voice.

"You made it, I'm happy to pour." Snagging another mug, he poured more fresh coffee and carried both mugs to the large oak table. "Looks like you're busy. Am I going to be in the way?"

"No." Chloe's voice was raspy. To cover it, she sipped the coffee, forgetting how hot it would be.

"Whew. Must have asbestos-lined innards." Shaking his head, Gordon added cream to his own mug.

Chloe placed one hand over her scalded mouth.

"Chloe? That burned, didn't it?" Rising, he grabbed a glass, put a few ice cubes and milk inside, and rushed it back. "Here, drink this. It'll help."

Obediently, she sipped the cold milk. It did help, but for the life of her, Chloe couldn't dredge up a smile.

Concerned, Gordon studied her. "It's not just the hot coffee. You look like you lost your best friend."

Realizing the milk was no disguise, she set it on the table. "No. Not my best friend."

Gordon leaned back in his chair. "Jimmy."

"I'm so pleased, beyond pleased, that Evan has finally accepted Jimmy as his own." Chloe lifted her face, fierceness burning in her eyes. "And I wouldn't change that for anything in the world."

"And you?"

"I've done my job." Expelling a deep breath, she looked back down.

"It hasn't been a job for you for quite a while now." Gordon squeezing her hand encouragingly. "And, it's not over."

"Afraid it is. I won't lie and say it's not killing me to leave Jimmy."

Gordon's kind, wise eyes searched hers. "Just Jimmy?"

"There's that wishful thinking bug again."

"Oh, Chloe. You've been able to see so much, learn so much while you've been here. Don't stop now."

She couldn't make Evan love her. Certainly couldn't make him stop missing his late wife, nor could she ever take Robin's place. And she couldn't say any of that to Gordon. "Thank you for the milk. I'd have never thought of it for a burned mouth."

He squeezed her hand again, then released it, leaning back to sip his cooling coffee. Chloe was grateful he didn't press her any longer. She couldn't bear it.

By five o'clock that afternoon, the Mitchell family had assembled in the entry hall. Everyone wore warm coats, gloves and hats. Chloe wore her warmest slacks and shirt, covered by the sweater she'd brought.

Evan turned the knob on the front door, then paused, turning around. "Whoops. Jimmy, I think we forgot something."

Jimmy nodded enthusiastically. "Uh-huh." He pulled out a small, gaily wrapped package, then handed it to Chloe. "Surprise!"

"It's a family tradition," Gordon explained. "Everyone gets to open a gift on Christmas Eve."

Chloe looked around. No one else was opening presents. But she didn't want to appear ungracious. With Jimmy about to burst, she unwrapped the box, peeled back the tissue paper and found a lovely pair of brown leather gloves.

"You can put 'em on now!" Jimmy urged, still smiling brightly.

"Great time for it," she agreed.

"I'll snip the tags," Thelma offered, producing a pair of scissors.

They had planned well.

"While she's doing that, open this one." Gordon handed her another box.

"You said *one* gift."

"One, two, who's counting?"

"You guys…" This time, she unwrapped a snug-looking ivory hat. "Very well coordinated, very appreciated. Thank you, Gordon."

Thelma held out a slim, rectangular package.

"Thelma, not you, too!"

"Open it or we're going to be late," Thelma instructed gruffly, her eager eyes giving away her pleasure.

A hand-knitted scarf in an array of colors from a golden caramel to deep brown rested in the folds of tissue paper. "Oh, Thelma... It's gorgeous. You must have spent hours making this."

"A body's got to stay warm," Thelma replied, trying unsuccessfully to disguise her delight.

Impulsively, Chloe hugged the older woman, who returned the gesture with a fierce hug of her own. "Guess I'd better put it on," Chloe said shakily, looping the lovely scarf around her neck. "Wow. I'm all set."

"Not quite," Evan objected.

Chloe wasn't sure where he'd hidden the large box he now extended to her. "Evan?"

"Just an early gift."

Hands trembling, she slipped off the silver ribbons, then unwrapped the delicate mauve and silver paper. Still shaking, she lifted the lid and set it aside. Chloe was almost afraid to open the pale pink tissue paper that nestled the gift. With everyone looking on, she pushed back the paper. Reverently, she smoothed one hand over the soft material inside. A winter-white cashmere coat, almost too beautiful to wear.

"Let's see it," Gordon encouraged.

Carefully picking it out of the box, she held it up

for everyone to see. A circle of pleased, enchanted faces met hers.

"It's not just for looking," Evan reminded her, gently taking the coat from her hands, holding it for her to put on.

Chloe slid one arm into a sleeve, turned to get the other. Evan fitted it in place, his hand lingering on her arm. Even though she tried not to, she glanced up as he stood so very close. His eyes burned with something she'd never before seen in them.

The little group was quiet as they watched and waited, but Chloe still couldn't break her gaze with Evan.

"Do you like it?" Jimmy asked, unable to contain his excitement any longer.

"It's…" Chloe cleared her throat, bogged down in emotion so rich it filled each of her senses, seemed to exude from every pore. "It's beautiful. The most beautiful gift I've ever received."

Evan remained silent, watching.

Chloe gradually returned to earth, then caught sight of her tight circle. "All of the gifts, I mean." She touched the scarf. "I've never received such a bounty of thoughtful, generous, lovely gifts. Thank you…everyone."

The live nativity was a highlight of Rosewood's Christmas celebration. A rural community, they had privy to all the animals that must have attended that first holy night.

Shepherds, along with the three wise men, flanked the stable. Mary and Joseph looked to the crêche.

"There's no one in the crib," Jimmy whispered to Evan.

"Because Jesus was born on Christmas Day," Evan explained. "This is the night before, when everyone waited for him."

"Oh." Jimmy watched the adults portraying Mary and Joseph. "Is that His mommy and daddy?"

"His earthly parents," Evan replied, knowing Jimmy would learn the full meaning in time.

Jimmy gripped his hand. "Are you my earthly daddy now? Since my first daddy's in heaven?"

Evan felt his love for Jimmy swell. "Yes."

"Then is Chloe my earthly mommy?"

Evan hoped so. With every fiber of being, he hoped to convince her to stay. He'd seen her shutting down, withdrawing. But he couldn't blow this chance. The Lord had given him a second family, and, in His wisdom, left that last chore to Evan. Kneeling down, he whispered close to Jimmy's ear, "That's what we need to pray for tonight. You understand?"

Jimmy nodded fervently, then whispered back, "I love Chloe."

His eyes misted, but Evan controlled his voice. "I love her, too."

Standing back up, his hands remained on Jimmy's

shoulders as they joined the crowd in singing "Silent Night."

One of the deacons, Robert Conway, began to read from the second chapter of Luke. "And, lo, the angel of the Lord came upon them, and the glory of the Lord shone...."

The familiar words washed over Evan as he silently prayed for just one more glorious event.

Chapter Seventeen

Having left the lights on, the Mitchell house looked warm and welcoming as they returned from the live nativity. Chloe had attended similar services before, but this one touched her deeply, knowing she had so much to be grateful for.

Following the others, she wondered why Gordon and Evan were walking toward the front while Thelma and Ned disappeared inside the back door. Since Jimmy held tightly to her hand, Chloe let him choose the course.

As usual, the door wasn't locked. Once inside, Chloe glanced down at her warm coat, unable to resist touching the sleeve one more time. While she did, Jimmy unclasped her hand. The room seemed unusually quiet. Lifting her gaze, Chloe stared straight ahead. A wing-backed chair that normally resided in the parlor had been moved to the hall. Gordon and

Evan stepped aside in opposite directions, revealing the chair's occupant.

Tears blurred Chloe's vision. "Mom?"

"Merry Christmas, sweetheart."

Chloe rushed across the hall, burying her face against her mother's shoulder as she had done as a child. Barbara stroked her daughter's hair, patted Chloe's back.

Raising her head, Chloe shook it in disbelief. "How…."

Barbara smiled gently. "Your friends. Grace's Aunt Ruth flew up to Milwaukee to get me. Then we flew back together and she drove us here."

Thoughts whirling, Chloe studied her anxiously. "Your oxygen?"

"I used the portable concentrator while we traveled. Grace's husband arranged for a home concentrator that the Mitchells put in a room for me."

"We have a guest suite downstairs on this floor," Gordon explained. "Set it up for my mother when she couldn't climb the stairs anymore. Had it renovated so it's got everything she might need."

Despite her joy, Chloe couldn't shed her anxiety. "And, you're really okay, Mom?"

"I'm better than okay." Barbara smiled tenderly. "I'm with my family for Christmas."

Turning to Evan and Gordon, Chloe looked at them for answers. "How did you arrange all this?"

"Well, now," Gordon began. "First of all, it

was all Evan's idea. He's had it planned since..."
Gordon scratched his head. "Better than two weeks,
I believe."

Chloe's gaze settled solely on Evan, her voice low.
"Weeks?"

Meeting her gaze, he nodded, his own dark eyes
still filled with that unidentified emotion.

"How did you even know how to contact my
mother?"

Grace's Aunt Ruth walked toward her from the
side of the hall where Thelma and Ned were also
standing. "Grace said she had a time coaxing the
name of the care facility from you."

Totally overwhelmed, Chloe couldn't take it in.
"Grace?"

"Evan called her to help him arrange everything.
She talked to me. Next thing we knew, your mother
and I were having a fine time traveling back to Rosewood. Didn't we, Barbara?"

"Very fine," Barbara agreed brightly.

"I don't know what to say," Chloe began, then
paused. "Yes, I do. Earlier, I thought I'd received
the most beautiful gift ever." She looked directly at
Evan, mentally urging him to understand. "I was
wrong. *This* is the most beautiful gift. And the most
special anyone has ever given me."

While the others talked in low rumbling voices,

she watched Evan's eyes. While she still couldn't read his thoughts, she sensed he understood her gratitude. And perhaps even more.

After Barbara had changed and climbed into bed, Chloe sat on the edge of the mattress, holding her mother's hand. "You took your nighttime medicine, right?"

"You've triple-checked all my meds and both oxygen machines. I feel wonderful, sweetheart."

"You look good," Chloe admitted. "Sorry to fret so, but honestly, Mom, you continue to amaze me."

Barbara chuckled quietly. "And you don't?"

Surprised, Chloe waited for her to continue.

"Sweetheart, you've made a whole new town full of friends, a new family—"

"Whoa. Friends, yes. And the Mitchells treat me wonderfully. But *you're* my family."

"Family grows, expands. That's how it's supposed to be."

Chloe swallowed, unwilling to worry her mother. Jimmy was Evan's now. And Evan…wasn't hers. "I'm so glad you're here. I have so much to tell you." They had already been talking nonstop for more than an hour after the group scattered and they were left alone. Chloe glanced at the clock on the nightstand. "But, it's late. You must be tired after the trip and all the excitement. I know I am."

"You know me too well."

Kissing her forehead, Chloe then rose. "Evan's sleeping in Jimmy's room tonight on the spare bed. So I'll be in the next room." The Mitchells still had a bed in the tiny adjoining space where a nurse had once stayed. Anticipating Chloe's intention, Thelma had made up the single bed. She had also brought down pajamas, robe, Chloe's best dress and all her gear from the upstairs bathroom.

"Honey, I don't want to cause more trouble for anyone."

"Trouble?" Chloe swallowed against tears of truth. "You have never been a moment's trouble, Mom. I wouldn't have things any other way. Sleep well."

"You too, sweetheart."

She turned the dimmer to low, then eased into the spare single bed. Knowing the Lord had differing paths for everyone, Chloe was grateful to have her mother here. It was going to be difficult enough to leave. It would help having Mom by her side.

Still, Chloe couldn't quash the pain that cratered in her heart as she thought of leaving Evan and Jimmy. Burying her face in her pillow, she muffled the sound. And wept into the night.

Christmas morning arrived with a flurry of motion and noise. At midday, the same group of people who had come to Thanksgiving would assemble for dinner, adding to the bustle.

First, as the clear, cloudless day dawned, Gordon gave thanks for His son, the gift of life, and gratitude for all those gathered in the parlor.

"Lovely prayer," Barbara told Gordon as the quiet amens rounded the room.

"We have been blessed beyond measure," he replied, glancing at his son and Jimmy on one side, Chloe on the other.

"I see that."

Chloe hoped her mother didn't see too much. "I just remembered. I mailed all your gifts!"

"And Ruth packed them in my spare suitcase." Barbara pointed to a portion of the gifts spilling over the needlepoint tree skirt. "Now, they're right here."

"I still can't believe I didn't catch on."

Barbara grinned. "That's why they're called surprises, dear."

Her mother's always optimistic, cheerful attitude was contagious. "Best one I've had."

Evan knelt down, retrieving packages, reading the names to Jimmy, who passed them around. Soon, everyone was digging into their gifts.

Chloe hoped her simple, inexpensive gifts weren't too shabby. Everyone else had been so generous.

Just then, Thelma held up the lace-trimmed linen handkerchief. "My goodness! This is a beauty. And just what I need. Now, I have a hankie nice enough to carry to church."

Pleased, Chloe watched tentatively as Ned pulled out his dress gloves.

"Me, too. Gloves, I mean, not a hankie. I can wear these to church."

"And cover up those leathery hands," Thelma added, then leaned over to kiss her husband's cheek.

Gordon was equally pleased with his gift.

Jimmy ripped the paper from his present. Chloe hoped he wasn't expecting a toy or video game. But when the bible was revealed, he smiled. Then he rushed over for a huge hug. "Thanks."

Chloe fought tears, wanting to never let him go. "I'm glad you like it, sweetheart."

"I can take my present to church, too!" Then he scrambled down, returning to Evan's side.

Evan opened presents from Ned and Thelma, then reached for Chloe's. Holding her breath, she waited for an excruciating few moments while he unwrapped it.

Once out of the box, Evan palmed the paperweight, examining all the edges.

"It's a paperweight," she explained. "Well, I guess you can see that. It's made out of limestone from your quarry. I guess you can see that, too," Chloe babbled, unable to stop the growing flow of words. "You probably have everything in the world a person can make from limestone, and out of your own quarry, too. I just thought, since you have an office, and then the study, here, maybe you could use one." Eventually, the flow reduced to a trickle. "Or not."

"I don't have another thing in my life like it." Again his eyes took on that unusual intensity, one she hadn't yet deciphered. His voice deepened. "Thank you."

Barbara patted Chloe's shoulder.

Evan handed her a small, slim box. "Merry Christmas."

Baffled, Chloe drew her eyebrows together. "But you already gave me my present."

"Just open it."

Trying not to let the shaking of her hands show, she opened the gift. Inside was a string of beads which matched her eyes. Stunned, she lifted the exquisite necklace. "Evan, it's beautiful! But it's too much!"

"Not for you."

She caressed the smooth, hand-carved jade. "Thank you."

The bustle continued, the noise level escalating. Yet all Chloe could hear were Evan's words, and wondered what they meant.

The dining room table was crowded with people. A second table held more, just as it had on Thanksgiving. But Perry volunteered to move so that Barbara could sit next to Chloe.

Although Evan would have liked to sit beside

Jimmy, he remained in his usual chair at the opposite end where he could view everyone. Barbara was even nicer than he'd hoped. He could see the resemblance, physical and personality-wise with Chloe. True to her word, Barbara hadn't breathed a word of his surprise. Chloe's expression had been worth every phone call, every niggling detail.

Now, though, Chloe's expression was no longer happy. Eating little, she alternately clasped her mother's and Jimmy's hands. Evan knew he hadn't voiced his feelings for her yet, but surely she sensed how he felt. Did she need a sign?

A sign as clear as the one he had received? A glint on Jimmy's handlebars on a sunless day shrouded in dark gray clouds? An explosion that could have taken them all?

Or just the words he had locked in his heart? Even there they stumbled. How could he possibly pour everything he felt into mere words?

"Great dinner as always," the elderly man on his right said, his hand shaky as he held on to his water glass.

"Thanks, Elmer. Glad you're enjoying it. How 'bout you, Clem? Getting enough to eat?"

"And then some, Evan." Clem lifted his fork in approval, his hand not shaking quite as much. But then he was two years younger than Elmer. Both were past ninety.

Evan could picture himself growing that old with Chloe at his side. But first, he acknowledged silently, he had to say the words.

After dinner ended, guests lingered for a while, then gradually dispersed to their own homes. This was usually Chloe's favorite time of day. The five of them had retreated to the parlor. Thelma threatened to lock the kitchen door if any of them, other than Ned, tried to help her clean the kitchen and wash dishes.

The fire burned at just the right level, warming the room, the flames dimly lighting rather than jumping. The short stack of logs in the oversize fireplace spit occasionally, then retreated to a comforting crackle. And Barbara was within a hand's reach. Jimmy sat at her feet, playing a new video game Gordon had given him. The tree, still redolent of its fresh pine boughs, twinkled in the early evening.

Mom and Gordon were getting on well, enjoying each other as contemporaries. It occurred to Chloe that having people one's own age to talk with was important. Her mother was in her late fifties. Most of the people in her care facility were much older. Did she miss having friends her own age close by? She would have to check into that once they were back.

The pain jabbed again as it had each time Chloe thought of returning to Milwaukee. The city had always been her home. Now she felt like she was being shipped to the far edges of the planet.

Jimmy jumped up. "I'm gonna go get the picture of me in the play and show it to your mommy."

"She'll like that." Chloe watched him scamper out of the room, his energy apparently boundless.

"I hate to put an end to a wonderful day, but I think I'll go to bed," Barbara said. "Jimmy can bring the picture to my room."

"I'll help—"

Barbara waved away the offer. "I can get there on my own. Stay, enjoy yourself." Clutching her small, light oxygen carrier, she left.

Worried, Chloe watched.

"She's only one room away," Gordon reminded her gently. "But she's got the right idea. I'm done in myself. Good night, young people."

Achingly aware that only she and Evan remained in the parlor, Chloe drew herself up, trying to disappear in the depths of the chair.

Evan rose and grabbed a poker, stirring the deteriorating fire. "Your mother's a fine woman."

"You won't get an argument out of me."

Replacing the poker, he turned. "Is that a promise?"

Chloe stared at him, the only sound between them the lingering, last gasp crackling of the fire.

"How come your suitcase is packed?" Jimmy demanded, running to a stop in front of her.

"What?"

"I saw it!" His lips wobbled. "On your bed. Like you're going somewhere."

"Jimmy, Evan's going to be your guardian. You have a wonderful home here with him."

"But why are *you* going?"

Evan walked close. "Yeah. I'd like to know that myself."

She gaped at him. "What?"

"I said I want to know why you're leaving."

Chloe gestured haplessly at Jimmy, silently imploring Evan to help her. But he didn't.

"My job's done. You know that."

"Nuh-uh," Jimmy protested. "*I'm* not done."

Again, Chloe beseeched Evan with her eyes.

He shrugged. "Jimmy's right. We're not done with you." Evan walked to within inches of her chair. In a swift movement he pulled her up from the chair, holding her next to him.

Chloe's throat was dry, clogged. "You're not?"

"Are you arguing with us?" Evan asked, his face so close to hers, she could see the depths of his eyes, could feel the whisper of his breath.

"I…." Words failed to pass through the acres of emotion crammed into the small space of her throat.

"Chloe, will you stay? Marry me? Mother Jimmy? Make us a family?"

The heat of his breath eased over her cheek, hovered near her mouth. "Marry?"

"Yes!" Jimmy jumped up and down. "Marry us!"

"I want to."

"That's all I need to hear." Evan cradled the back of her head, his fingers laced between strands of her hair.

"But I can't."

For a moment the room silenced. Not even the fire dared make a sound.

"Why not?" Evan demanded, his face so close to hers she could feel the thrust of his chin against hers.

"My mother. I can't leave her." The dam of emotion burst, flooding her heart, spilling her tears. "You don't understand. I've never wanted anything so much, to be with you, to have Jimmy as my own, but I can't! Don't make me choose!"

"You don't have to choose."

Confused, Chloe shook her head. "Of course I do. I'll never leave my mother on her own."

"What if your mother moves to Rosewood? In here with us?"

"Here? She has to have someone in the house with her all the time. She can't—"

"There's always someone here," he replied gently. "Thelma, Ned, my dad, you, me, Jimmy. And, if by some miracle, not one of us can be here, we have lots of friends and neighbors who can help."

Did she really dare hope? Muddled, she tried to think of all the reasons it wouldn't work. "My mother might not *want* to live here."

"Funny. She told me she'd be very happy to move to Rosewood, to be close to you and your family."

"But, when—"

"When I knew, *finally* knew, I couldn't live without you. Barbara's excited by the idea. You two can spend a lot more time together that way. Unless you really want to go to law school?"

"Law school?" she echoed. "Why... No, I don't care about going to law school. That was just a way to support my mother. And Mr. Wainwright was going to pay..." Chloe stopped abruptly. "Does this mean you trust me now? Really trust me?"

Evan took her hand and placed it on his chest. "With all my heart."

She felt tears slipping down her face. Evan carefully, gently eased them away with his thumb as he had once before. He touched her lips with the same thumb, tracing their outline. Angling his head, he claimed her lips, sealing their promise with his own.

Sated, Evan pulled back slightly. "Is that a yes?"

Breathless, she spoke against the fullness of his lips. "Yes! Definitely, yes!"

"Yes!" Jimmy hollered, jumping beside them.

Bailey barked, circling them with his tail wagging.

Yes, my love. Yes.

"How did we ever put a wedding together this fast?" Chloe asked her matron of honor.

Grace shrugged. "Helps having a wedding gown designer right on Main Street who could whip up a dress." The owner of the shop had jumped in to help, finishing a winter-white gown she had already begun sewing. "Not to mention the Conway Nursery growing flowers all year round." They had chosen deep burgundy roses, creamy calla lilies and hand-gathered swags of evergreen. The owner of the local bakery hadn't even blinked when asked to produce a fully decorated wedding cake. Grace swished the skirt of her long, emerald green gown. "Didn't hurt that I had my own dress, too."

"And I was already in town," Barbara added with a twinkle in her eye.

"I can't believe Ruth talked you into bringing your best dress."

Grace chuckled. "We just seem mild. Our family's actually pretty ruthless."

Ruthless in running every errand, delivering invitations by hand, arranging with the pastor to have the church on New Year's Eve morning, collecting candles to light the sanctuary, enlisting friends with catering and decorating skills.

Mindful of the dress's large train, Chloe turned to her mother. "Are you really sure? Really, really sure you want to move here?"

Barbara threw back her head, laughing. "Good thing I have plenty of oxygen with me. Yes, my dear, for the thousandth time, I am absolutely, positively, one hundred and ten percent sure. Why wouldn't I be? I can see you every day, watch my grandson grow up."

Chloe smiled, thinking of how instantly Jimmy had bonded with her.

"And," Barbara continued, "you're happy. Truly happy. Do you know how long I've wanted that for you?"

Tears misted.

"Now don't start that," Barbara insisted. "Or I'll be weeping buckets."

Grace sniffled. "Me, too."

Chloe turned back to the mirror, wiping her eyes with the newly embroidered hankie Thelma had pressed in her hand that morning. Her new initials, CMM, were stitched in blue on the cotton square. Something blue.

She had piled her tamed curls on top of her head, securing them before adding a delicate headband encrusted with pearls that Grace provided. Something borrowed.

Barbara rolled forward in her wheelchair, then extended her hand, holding a single strand of heirloom pearls. "I wore these on my wedding day, and so did your grandmother."

Touched, Chloe picked up the delicate necklace. "But how did you know?"

"Ruth was *very* helpful," Barbara said with a straight face. Then her lips trembled, giving away her feelings.

Chloe reached down to hug her tightly. "Thank you, Mom."

"You'll pass them down to your daughter one day."

"Daughter?" Beautiful thought. Chloe put them to her neck and fastened the clasp. Something old.

Grace held out a small jewelry box.

"Grace, what—"

"Just open it," Grace chided gently.

Overwhelmed, Chloe opened the case, revealing a pair of pearl earrings. Ones that were the same shade as the aged pearl necklace. "I've never seen anything like this. Not just that you've planned so perfectly, coordinated it beyond belief, but your generosity. Everyone's."

Grace smiled. "I'm glad they match so well."

Fastening them to each earlobe, Chloe blinked away another threat of tears. Something new.

Notes from the organ floated into the bride's room. Chloe turned, facing Grace and her mother. "Sounds like the music before the main event."

Noah knocked on the door. "Grace? Susie's ready."

Grace's husband had watched their daughter, who was to be the flower girl, while the women helped Chloe dress. Accustomed to being quiet in church, five-year-old Susie held her basket obediently, shyly smiling.

Jimmy wasn't to be the ring bearer, though. Evan had chosen him to be the best man, to stand beside them while they exchanged vows.

Gordon had agreed to walk Chloe down the aisle. She had been torn, wishing her mother was strong enough for the task. But Barbara insisted she preferred to sit in the traditional position of the bride's mother in the front pews.

Barbara broke into her thoughts. "I'd better go. I'll need that extra bit of time." One of the ushers was going to help her into the pew, then move her wheelchair to the foyer until after the service concluded.

Chloe bent, kissing her mother's soft cheek. "I love you, Mom."

Barbara met her gaze. "You are the dearest daughter in the world. Be happy, Chloe."

Grace adjusted the simple satin bow on Susie's pale green dress. Then she knelt to check Chloe's train on the whipped up dress. A vintage-inspired satin and tulle Cinderella gown with a sweetheart neckline, fitted bodice, long sleeves and a chapel-length train that spread out behind her elegantly.

Chloe clutched her bouquet of hand-tied, deep red calla lilies. "It's *really* real."

"You look beautiful," Grace murmured.

"Because I have a beautiful friend."

Grace looked ready to choke up. Instead, she blinked away the tears and took her daughter's hand. "Ready, ladies?"

Rosewood's Community Church was more than one hundred and fifty years old. The intricate stained-glass windows allowed the morning sunlight to illuminate the hand-tooled wooden pews, the clusters of fresh roses and calla lilies, and the guests in the congregation. The sunbeams' warmth coaxed the fragrance of both the roses and evergreens to scent the air. Candles flickered in arched brass holders flanking the nave.

Gordon met Chloe in the marbled foyer. "You look beautiful, *daughter*."

She took his arm, clinging to him for support. "So do you."

Grace knelt down beside Susie when the ushers opened the tall, wide doors to the sanctuary. "Now, sweetheart."

The delicate girl, who looked so much like her mother, took small, careful steps as she dropped red rose petals on the wide center aisle.

Grace smiled brightly, then turned and followed her daughter. When she reached the altar, the organ music grew louder as it began trumpeting the traditional wedding march.

Chloe stepped around the door, seeing the fully decorated church for the first time.

Gordon squeezed her hand and whispered, "Ready?"

Nodding, Chloe took the deepest breath of her life. They started up the aisle when she saw her mother stand, the traditional custom to signal the rest of the guests to do likewise. Looking into the faces of the guests, she realized many of them were familiar. From school, church, the office, even the holiday dinners. Nearing her mother, Chloe met her proud, pleased gaze. Then she met another set of eyes.

And was glad she had taken that deep breath because she thought she might not be able to take another.

Evan stood tall and proud. His thick, wavy hair had been tamed, his crisp white shirt emphasized his tanned, compelling features. That strong, stubborn jaw, aristocratic nose, those mesmerizing midnight-colored eyes.

Without effort, Chloe glided from Gordon's arm to Evan's. Turning toward him, she thought she might drown within the emotions written on his face.

The pastor began speaking and while Chloe listened, she caught Jimmy's attention, sending him a smile his very own.

"Will you, Chloe Marie Reed, take this man, Evan

Sean Mitchell, to be your lawfully wedded husband, to have and to hold from this day forward, for better or worse, for richer, for poorer, in sickness and in health, to love and to cherish from this day forward until death do you part?"

This time nothing crowded her throat or conviction. "I do."

The familiar words continued, seeming to fly by as fast as the wedding preparations themselves.

"I now pronounce you husband and wife. You may kiss the bride."

Chloe felt Evan's tender kiss lingering. Then he took her hand, caressing the engagement ring he had presented her, one that had been his mother's. He had purchased a new wedding band to slide beside it, to signify their new union.

Again the organ music soared, all stops pulled out. They turned to greet their loved ones.

"Mr. and Mrs. Evan Mitchell," the pastor announced.

They stepped down the wide, wooden stairs. Chloe looked up at her new husband. Reading the request in her eyes, they paused at her mother's pew. Embracing her, Chloe gave thanks for all the Lord was showering upon them.

Gordon rose from the other side of the aisle, extending a hand to Jimmy, then crossing over to wait with Barbara while the new couple continued down the aisle and out into the foyer.

Thelma mopped her face with her new handkerchief and Ned reached over to borrow the damp hankie.

Chloe and Evan could only see each other and the love that flowed as swiftly as the now fast-moving river. Because winter had officially arrived in Rosewood. Just as Chloe had done.

Before dashing out to a shower of soap bubbles and confetti, Evan took her hand, pulled her close. "That was I *do* I heard back there?"

Her lips eased into a wide smile before meeting his. "Yes. Most definitely yes."

Tender, possessive, protective, Evan's kiss reflected all.

"I love you, Mrs. Mitchell."

The future opened in front of them like a fertile hill country meadow. "And, I love you, Mr. Mitchell. One more promise?"

"Anything."

"Tell me again on our fiftieth anniversary."

Evan's smile flashed, his eyes full of tenderness. "Don't make me wait *that* long."

Their laughter blended like the vines of a climbing rose, then was muted by the kiss that sealed their promise. And grew to the skies.

Epilogue

The following Christmas

Jimmy Mitchell hovered over his two-month-old baby sister, tucking on a teeny pink bootie she had kicked off. "Gracie won't keep her socks on."

Chloe and Evan exchanged an amused glance while Gordon snapped a photo of the quartet that now made a complete, loving family.

"That's so you'll keep checking on her, son." Evan crossed over to the cradle.

Obviously pleased, Jimmy shrugged. "In that case, it's okay."

Evan ruffled his hair. "And that's what makes you a good big brother."

"I'll say so," Gordon chimed in. "And that's what every little girl needs."

Barbara spread open her arms. "How about a hug for Grandma?"

Jimmy ran over, fitting into her big hug. Barbara's face glowed when he perched on her lap. Her health had been improving steadily the past year and she hadn't had pneumonia once during that time. Grace's husband, Noah, had connected them with an excellent pulmonary specialist and Barbara's health was better than it had been in a decade. She still had COPD, but the dry hill country weather was far healthier for her than the humidity in Milwaukee, a city bisected by a river and bounded by one of the great lakes.

Chloe had tried not to worry, but it was a longtime habit, difficult to break. So Evan called in an electrician who had installed alarm buttons in Barbara's suite. Chloe ordered a medical alert necklace that Barbara always wore, but hadn't needed to use.

Gordon captured Barbara and Jimmy in another shot. Gordon and Barbara had become good friends as well, generously sharing their grandson. Together, they had surprised Chloe and Evan by decorating the house for the holidays with both white and burgundy-red calla lilies, boughs of evergreen, and deep burgundy roses, reminiscent of their holiday wedding.

The living Christmas tree was even taller, filled with all the traditional ornaments and sporting new ones for both Jimmy and Gracie. Jimmy had two, one proclaiming him the best big brother, the other declaring him the most beloved son. Gordon and Barbara had collaborated on a small wreath for Jimmy's bedroom door. Instead of pinecones or the normal greenery, they made it from similarly sized replicas of sports balls—soccer, basketball, baseball, football. And, an emblem at the base announced that he was their number one grandson.

Sensitive to Gordon's late grandson, Sean, Barbara had suggested a different phrasing, but Gordon insisted. Jimmy needed all their love and support in his new family.

For Gracie, a tiny pair of pink porcelain booties were inscribed with her name, date of birth. Chloe watched as she and Jimmy gooed at each other. Her heart was so full, she was surprised it didn't burst.

Jimmy and Evan had bonded so tightly, no one would ever guess he was adopted. Chloe had taken him into her heart even sooner and Jimmy was truly hers in every way. He had blossomed as well in the previous year. She and Evan had adopted him immediately after their honeymoon in San Antonio.

Neither had wanted to travel far, and few other places were as romantic as the nearly century-old walkways nestled against the banks of the San Antonio River, a story below the city itself. Magical year round, it was a fantasy during the holidays. Festooned with twinkling white lights, the waterway carried boats that glided slowly beneath bridges, evoking a sense of incomparable romance. Not that Evan and Chloe needed the setting.

She glanced at her husband of one year, still marveling that he was hers. His pain had subsided after he placed it in the Lord's hands. Renewing his faith had revived his life, his generous heart, his willingness to love without boundaries.

Someone rapped the knocker on the front door. It was still fairly early on Christmas Day, but the family had opened all their presents. Most visitors wouldn't arrive until their traditional midday meal.

Thelma hopped up first. "Early for guests." She opened the door, her tone changing completely. "Well, come on in."

Chloe recognized her best friend's voice. Grace, her aunt Ruth, Noah and Susie chattered while they strolled into the parlor.

"Merry Christmas!" Chloe rose from the sofa. "I didn't know we'd get to see you today!"

"And miss my namesake's first Christmas?" Grace replied with a swift hug. "Ah, there she is!" Grace walked quickly to the cradle, stopping first to greet Jimmy. "Hey, big brother. You still liking your sister?"

"Yeah." Jimmy ducked his head. "She's okay."

Grace grinned. "Going to keep her then?"

"Uh-huh."

Reaching the cradle, Grace peered down. "I'm not quite sure how we managed to have the three most beautiful children in the world." The baby held up one hand and Grace offered her pinky finger which Gracie latched on to. "She's getting really strong."

Susie tiptoed next to her mother. Fascinated, she stared into the cradle. "Is our baby going to be that little?"

Chloe stared at her friend, hoping Grace's prayer had been answered.

Grace patted her still flat tummy. "I imagine so."

Chloe rushed to give her a hug, while Evan pumped Noah's hand in congratulation.

"Ruth Stanton!" Barbara declared. "Why didn't you tell me?"

"Promised I wouldn't," Ruth replied with an apologetic shrug and nod toward her niece.

Barbara and Ruth had become fast friends. Ruth urged Barbara to join the ladies auxiliary and picked her up each week to attend the meetings. In between, they had lunches both out in town and in the house. Many afternoons were spent playing dominos, gin rummy or hearts. Barbara still had to carry her portable concentrator, but Ruth treated it as just an extra purse. They had purchased a power scooter so Barbara could *walk* through town with her friend.

And, as Evan had predicted, they had yet to need extra help to ensure someone was always in the house with Barbara. Using the lighter wheelchair Chloe had suggested, it was always easy to pack the chair in the back of a car. So Barbara attended church regularly, including special events like the live nativity the previous evening.

Barbara winked at Ruth. "I'm happy for all of you." The much prayed for pregnancy was a blessing Grace and Noah had wanted for some time.

"Between us, we'll have four little ones to spoil." Ruth patted Susie's back.

"And I'm the oldest," Jimmy bragged.

"You sure are, big guy." Evan scooped him up, flinging him up over his head, making Jimmy giggle.

The blessings continued to flow, Chloe thought. Mitchell Stone had revived due to the large order they had been able to produce. Everyone's jobs were safe. The company was doing so well that Melanie, the woman Chloe had stepped in for, didn't have to return to work. Instead, they were able to hire her husband for a different position and Melanie was ecstatic to be home with her children.

Grace reluctantly retrieved her hand when the baby's eyes closed. "She gets prettier every day."

"Just like her godmother." Chloe and Evan had readily agreed to name the baby after Chloe's best friend because, without her, they might not have had a happy ending. Grace had been pivotal in negotiating the tricky issues that divided them. And, she'd been instrumental in successfully bringing Barbara to Rosewood. Grace had filled Ruth in on everything so that Barbara would be prepared for what she was walking into.

"Do you suppose we've started a tradition?" Grace mused. "Having new babies for Christmas?"

"I can't imagine a better one." Chloe squeezed her friend's hand. "I'm so happy for you."

"I've pretty much been waltzing on air since I suspected. I just didn't want to say anything too soon."

"Your timing's perfect." She chuckled.

"What?"

"Just thinking that one day Gracie will wear Mom's pearls on her wedding day, too."

"She's a bit young," Grace teased.

Chloe rubbed the emerald ring on her right hand. Evan had given it to her when Gracie was born. For Christmas, she had received the matching earrings. He continued to spoil her and she loved every moment.

As though he knew her thoughts, Evan met her eyes from across the room. It had been that way since their wedding day, their unspoken communication of each other's needs.

Weaving through their small crowd, speaking to guests on the way, Evan and Chloe met near the fragrant Christmas tree. There was one other ornament that also adorned the tree. A bride and groom, hand in hand, beside a manger cradling the holy babe.

The Lord had brought them together, blessed them beyond measure and continued to hold them in His hands. Looking around the room at all the dear faces, Chloe was so thankful she had to bite back a tear.

"What is it, my love?"

"I'm just so happy," she sniffled.

Evan took her hand, absently polishing the deep

green gemstone on her finger. "We've got a lot to be happy for." His life was changed forever. Hope replaced longing, love conquered pain. He put an arm around her waist. "I wasted a lot of time being angry."

She touched his cheek. "The Lord has plenty of patience."

"He needed it with me."

"He knew you were worth it." Chloe smiled tenderly. "So did I."

Evan kissed her long, slim fingers, warmed as always by the sight of the gold band encircling her left ring finger. *What if she hadn't persisted, had accepted his refusal?*

Chloe's hair fell long and loose, the waves cascading over her shoulders, resting full and thick on her back. He would always remember the first silky touch of her curls, the sight of her moonwashed lips, their softness when they kissed for the first time. "I love you more every day," he said quietly, so only she could hear. "No, every minute."

"You're determined to make me cry," she replied, placing her hand on his chest, atop the beat of his heart. "I believe this is mine."

"Always."

Gordon snapped his camera. "Now, I need you two over by Jimmy and Gracie."

Barbara had removed Gracie from the cradle, coaxing her awake with Jimmy's help.

Amused, Evan held his wife's hand as they approached their children. Sitting side by side on the couch, Evan plunked Jimmy on to his lap while Chloe held the baby.

"Smile," Gordon instructed.

Instinctively, Chloe and Evan turned to each other with tender smiles. Gracie cooed and Jimmy grinned.

Gordon clicked the camera, captured the moment. "Perfect picture."

"Perfect family," Evan replied.

He didn't mind as his father shepherded everyone into various groups for all the photos he wanted to take. Then Gordon set the timer and everyone crowded together for a shot of the entire family. Grace, Noah, Ruth and Susie were now family, too. They could fill a new album with just the ones Gordon would shoot this day.

Evan reached again for Chloe's hand. "Always," he murmured, lowering his mouth to hers. Not a whisper of air separated them. And Chloe leaned into his kiss, lingering, loving, wishing the moment would never end.

Just as their marriage. It had taken wing on the tail of the Christmas star. And, now, it glowed, growing brighter, stronger, more heavenly. "Always."

* * * * *

Dear Reader,

Like many of you, I've been caught in the excruciating position of being in one place, while needing to be in another. To be entangled in family and work in one state, while aging parents reside in another. They call us the Oreo generation for a reason, I suppose. More and more of us are dealing with our children growing into adults while our parents are reaching their twilight years, putting us in the middle. For me, it's not duty, it's love.

But love, as we also know, is tricky enough on its own. And, when it's new love, how do we make these crucial decisions?

I feel a special kinship with Chloe Reed as she must choose between love and family on opposite sides of the country. And, I hope you'll enjoy this venture to Rosewood as we're all reminded of how very special our families are. And, how much they love, give, inspire and challenge.

Blessings,

Bonnie K. Winn

QUESTIONS FOR DISCUSSION

1. How did you feel about Chloe leaving her mother in Milwaukee?

2. Taking a child across the country to a new home is fairly daunting. Would you ever consider doing anything similar?

3. Did you agree with Chloe's decision to accept her boss's offer?

4. Do you think Chloe should have placed Barbara in a lower-quality facility so that she didn't have so much financial pressure?

5. Should Chloe's younger brother have been urged to do more for their mother? Or, did you feel his primary obligation was to his wife and children?

6. Evan considered the stone company's employees to be family. Do you feel he was overly concerned about their welfare? Or did you admire his principles?

7. Evan's father, Gordon, opened their home to Chloe. Do you think he was right? Or should he have respected Evan's wishes?

8. Chloe's mother agreed to move to Rosewood. Do you think Barbara will be happy close to her daughter? Or will she feel she's left everything familiar behind?

9. In Barbara's position, what would you have done?

10. Can you understand Chloe's belief that she couldn't give Jimmy a good home on her own?

11. Do you think Evan should have given more consideration to Jimmy's grandparents' offer to put him in boarding school?

12. Grace, the heroine of *Promise of Grace*, overcame incredible difficulties. Do you think she has come full circle? Now giving back to the community that embraced her?

13. Is belief and love enough to bind a family? Are finances merely secondary considerations?

14. Can you imagine yourself living in a place completely different, perhaps even opposite, of your home? From big city to small town? Or vice versa?

15. How much would you be willing to sacrifice for your family? All the generations of your family?

LARGER-PRINT BOOKS!

**GET 2 FREE
LARGER-PRINT NOVELS
PLUS 2 FREE
MYSTERY GIFTS**

Larger-print novels are now available...